ADVANCE PRAISE

Tom Sheehan writes from the heart, with a soul that knows no leash
on depth. He lives with a richness, soaks in every ray of sunshine,
every raindrop, every glance exchanged and breath shared, each
touch a treasure, whether a sparkling gem or a twisted, ravaged
angst. We savor his storytelling like a slice of his grandmother's
buttered bread, warm from oven, and oh so belly soothing. He is the
Master, our Twenty-first century Great American writer.

-Diane Buccheri, Publisher, OCEAN Magazine

I might be the only person in Montana who knows Tom Sheehan, so
I feel obligated to fill in this blank. He's very American, a veteran of
the Korean War, and a long-time employee of Raytheon Company in
Massachusetts. He wins all sorts of prizes but the Big Five
publishers take no notice. Somehow he manages to write in an old-
fashioned plot vs. character way while all the time being curiously
modern. Hard to explain. He writes about shooting, horses and bad
guys -- all with extraordinary names and detail -- but he also
manages a poetic grasp of detail and landscape. He doesn't stay in
categories very well, but once he chooses his "method," he knows
what he's doing.

-Prairie Mary Scriver

The Cowboys

Thomas F. Sheehan

Pocol Press
Clifton, VA

POCOL PRESS
Published in the United States of America
by Pocol Press
6023 Pocol Drive
Clifton, VA 20124
www.pocolpress.com

Publisher's Cataloguing-in-Publication

Names: Sheehan, Thomas F., 1928-, author.
Title: The Cowboys / Thomas F. Sheehan.
Description: Clifton, VA: Pocol Press, 2016.
Identifiers: ISBN 978-1- 929763-69- 6 | LCCN 2016943772
Subjects: LCSH Ranchers--Fiction. | Ranch life--Fiction. | Frontier and pioneer life--West (U.S.)--Fiction. | Pony Express--Fiction. | Cowboys--Fiction. | Outlaws--Fiction. | West (U.S.)--Fiction. | Western stories. | Short stories, American. | Historical fiction. | BISAC FICTION / Westerns | FICTION / Short Stories (single author). Classification: LCC PS3569.H39216 C69 2016 | DDC 813.6--dc23

Library of Congress Control Number: 2016943772

ACKNOWLEDGEMENTS

Tom Sheehan's stories have appeared in *Rope and Wire Western Lifestyle Magazine, Western Online,* and *Literally Stories.*

Preface

This collection came into being in my industrious turn to continue working in a place very common for me, the handling of words and their complexions and complexities, how they shape and mold characters caught in the act of living in the midst of joy, sadness and resolutions. Nothing gives me more comfort than creating something somewhat new in a current environment, or one that I can envision as being, has been, or can be. Poetry, the sound in my bone and marrow, in the little room behind my eyeballs, in the constant whispering that I attend to from a variety of sources, some of them barely audible, keep me on the prowl, much like the night person I must be. Be it a poem of sorts, a western story or yesterday's news translated by my tongue and twist, the comfort becomes mine ... and hopefully yours, here and in other pages.

TABLE OF CONTENTS

Matt Durgin sat with his wife Grace on the porch of their ranch house, evening taking hold for good, the heat of the day still in place, the mountains to the west of them keeping months of rain away from the grass, the eventual winter feed for their animals.

Grace Durgin, at 35 a pretty blonde with a generally good outlook on ranch life and its ups and downs, said "What's for tomorrow, Matthew?" She lifted her eyes from knitting, saw her husband staring to see the last of the ranch in the shadows, with another deep reflection worry locking him up.

He didn't answer.

"Is it really that serious, Matt? We've been through tough times before."

"If we lose the fields," he said, "that means we lose winter feed and that means we'd have to sell off the animals. I hate that thought."

He put his hand out as if to measure the heat, the dryness, the near-drought, the full dangers and loss facing them.

Changing her approach to matters, she said, ""Have you seen how Timmy has grown these last few months? He's really sprouting."

It didn't work as intended, as her husband replied, "I sure wish the grass would grow the same way. Granton's sitting in town waiting for us to fold up and walk away, like he's seen so many do."

"Is he as bad as you say, Matt?" Her soft restraint did not work again.

"Oh, Gracie, don't be so innocent. He feeds on our losses, anybody out here on this far side of rain. He'd scoop up land, animals, and people if he could, just to build his little empire. He wants the whole range from here to Jehrico Springs, and he's already got Jehrico Springs." He paused to build up a known litany. "And Harmon's place and old George Tucker's and even that twist of land by the old fort. It's all his now."

He stopped talking when he heard his son Timmy singing, with a decent voice, in his room right off the porch.

His wife observed him shaking his head, making measurements, forming decisions.

"Timmy," he yelled, "come out and say goodnight. We've got

1

a big day tomorrow. C'mon now." He slapped his hand on the rail.

The round-faced, curly-headed 7-year old still wearing his boots came out the door and said, in his high-pitched voice, singing still gripping him, "I forgot to ask you something, Pa." He was bright as a new saddle, the boy, and his eyes set on his father's face, then on his mother's, but he managed to say what was working in him. In a curious, heightened voice, he said, "When I saw some men today, on the other side of the ravine, they were making things, a bunch of them, with a fire going and wrapping stuff on the end of tree branches, kind of straight ones like arrows, and then dipping them in a bucket they had sitting near the fire."

"Who was doing that, Timmy? You know any of them?"

"No, but I seen some of them going to Granton's spread before. The one with a stocking horse, but only three legs all white, and a big black and a gray so pretty I could kiss her."

Durgin coughed a small attention cough, raised his eyebrows when his wife looked at him, and asked his son, "What did those men do with those sticks, Timmy? Did they see you? Did they take those sticks away with them? Did you see them leave?"

"They stuck them all in under a ledge and covered them up. The bucket too, the black bucket that they stuck the sticks into."

"What were you doing that far away from the ranch, Timmy?"

"Oh, me and Trotter was just taking a ride and then I saw them when we was resting for a while and having a sandwich and an apple I had for him and me. We sat in the grove of trees near the ravine, 'cause we was out of the sun and it got hot."

"You could see all that they did right from those trees, son?"

"Yup, everything they did, like they didn't know anybody small as me was around."

Durgin said, "You did fine, son, but don't go out that way again. Those men are kind of suspicious and might want to steal one of our cows or one of our horses for themselves." He looked directly at his wife who had stopped her knitting to assimilate all that she had heard from her boy, and the interpretation given by her husband, knowing something was in the offing, something not for their best interests.

"Trotter did good, Pa. Never made a noise at all. Just stood in place like I did."

2

"I think your ma will give you another apple for Trotter if you ask her." He nodded at his wife and said, "I'll take a few boys with me and we'll mosey around out that way in the morning, see what's been fashioned for a surprise. That's what I'm guessing, it's supposed to be a big surprise."

His words came calmly, without any stress or conjecture to them, but his face was set for the course. She knew him so well, she could feel the urgency running through her frame, but she remained still, back to knitting, before she added, "Timmy and I will bake some of those cookies you really like, Matt. Won't we, Timmy?"

The three of them left the porch for their promised tasks, two to the kitchen, and one to the bunkhouse.

Durgin explained the situation to three of his crew, all trusted hands, all with him through the harsh times that had descended on them, and perhaps were being escalated by other than Mother Nature. He laid out a plan of approach in case there were any of the suspected men were about or the cache of sticks was uncovered by others, accidentally. They'd leave early in the morning.

The false dawn found them in the cluster of trees where Timmy Durgin had observed the suspicious group of men. Durgin directed two of his men toward each end of the ravine to watch for activity, such as riders, or anything that might disturb his intention of finding more about the situation.

"Duke and I will stay here for a while, keeping watch in case someone's around or keeping watch. Then we'll get over there directly. You two hightail it to each end of the ravine and watch the approach. Come back this way quick as you can. If you can't, and someone's bounden you shan't, fire two shots. That clear?"

The two men agreed and slipped off to do as bidden.

Durgin and his man Duke Prescott waited a while, saw no activity, rode down into the ravine and staked their horses. With little difficulty even while carrying their rifles, they climbed the other side of the ravine and came out directly in front of the overhanging ledge, a pile of brush under it, which Timmy had spoken about.

They pulled away the brush, saw the black bucket and a dozen sticks stacked in under the ledge, one end of each stick wrapped in rags and dipped in oil and tar, perfect tools for torches that would burn for a good while.

Prescott said as he looked at a pile of ashes, "There's been a

3

fire here, Matt; I'd guess they had heated up some of the tar to dip the sticks in after being soaked in oil. If there was any oil left, they dumped it, but hid the tar bucket. Couldn't throw that down the ravine. What cha think?" He was nodding before Durgin answered.

"They were gonna burn our grass, Duke. That's what they were up to. We only have Timmy's word on this, and what's here that could have been left by anybody. We got to get them in the loop of things. We damned well know Granton's behind this. I'd just love to catch him at it. Pin his ass to the wall one last time."

He looked back over his shoulder, to the spread of dry grass, all the way to the ranch proper. "If a fire got going good, it could get to the house and the barn with any wind in the kick of it." He kicked the ground, "Damned idiots."

A soft whistle came on a breath of air. Prescott said, "That's Ben Paulie, Matt. He's come back from the west end of the ravine, and look," he pointed to the clutch of trees, "he's back in there and pointing the way he was watching. Someone's coming. We'd best hide in the rocks here. Hope they don't see our horses."

The two men hid in amongst a tumble of rocks a long time in place from a rock eruption in the heart of the earth. It provided good protection for them.

Shortly, six riders came along the top of the ravine from the direction of town, and Granton's spread, Granton in the lead on his big gray. He was delivering orders before he even was dismounted, "Get that brush out of there and get a fire going so we can light them torches. We'll burn Durgin's fields so he has to pull out of here. He ain't gonna stand in my way. Get that fire goin', now." His voice was loud and nasty.

Prescott's hands were both on his rifle, as if he was about to shoot. Durgin touched him on the shoulder, put his finger to his lips to get both his silence and no action, and then slowly held his hand up to give the same kind of order to Ben Paulie across the ravine and in the clutch of trees.

Granton, still giving harsh orders, yelled, "Get that fire goin' good so's we can light these torches and burn Durgin right out of his holdins."

The brush was out from under the overhang, the sticks dipped in oil and tar retrieved, the fire beginning to flame higher, when Durgin, rifle in hand, stepped up from behind a rock and said, "You

4

ain't burning anybody out today, Granton. We got you covered. Drop your guns. You boys are on your way to jail."

Granton did not move, instead sat his horse cool and deliberate and said, "One man ain't gonna take us to jail, Durgin, and that's a promise."

He was surprised when Prescott stood up a dozen feet away from Durgin, from behind another huge boulder, and said, "He ain't alone, Granton, 'cause I'm here and I'm the best shot in this here whole possible shootin' match, of which you are the first target."

And from across the ravine, hearing all of it, Ben Paulie fired two shots in the air, yelled out, "We're over here, Boss, and they ain't gonna hurt us or burn us out today or any day. We got that all covered."

From the south end of the ravine came two more shots as the other Durgin man fired his rifle in answer.

Ben Paulie said, "The others are comin', Boss, all of them, and these fire starters are goin' to jail for sure."

In the middle of full realization of where he was at, seeing what was coming down on him, his big dreams at the very edge of a steep ravine, Granton went for his gun. Two of his men, in the flurry of that sudden action, did the same.

Prescott, with one round, took Granton right off his saddle, Durgin knocked off another man whose revolver was taking aim at him, and leveled him across his saddle with a dead-on shot. Ben Paulie fired into the rest of the men, his shots bouncing off the rocks near them, so that all available guns were rendered useless for the matter of a gun fight. The weapons of four men hit the ground.

Durgin yelled to Paulie, "Ben, you better go in to town and bring the sheriff out here. He's got to see all this stuff just waiting for him."

He'd have to be careful with young Timmy, he realized, lest the boy go running around looking for more adventures, playing crooks and sheriffs.

5

She was right, and pleading, when she said, "The storm is coming. We can't get out of here, not all of us. Take my boy with you. You have the only horse. Our horse broke his leg and we had to kill him, and then we ate a lot of him. Four of us can't make it on one horse, and my husband's sicker than I thought." She nodded at him, bundled in old rags, a heavy jacket and blanket parts, a sicker man I had not seen since the war. With cheekbones like two rocks on the trail, his eyes had stayed shut for more than two hours as she argued with me, finally winning her way. "Take the boy," she said again, "and give him some kind of life. Don't let him be vagabonds like us."

She was asking me for help, me a long-time drifter who did not have a home for a long time. Me and the boy, when I really looked at it, were in cahoots in all this, becoming saddle pards.

Their place was tight against the mountain, in a small meadow they figured to stake a claim on; the future was bright, the grass would grow and feed many animals, special crops would grow in the good earth. A ring of mountains ran around them; however, when the storms came, like the one she was telling me about, they'd be locked into the meadow with escape most difficult.

So I left, the boy John in my lap as I rode, my arms and a blanket around him, the skies getting darker, the storm coming down upon us sooner than I realized. The wind in less than an hour turned vicious. I had to get into the canyon maze, to get a share of the natural protection.

"Take my boy," kept sounding in my head. I wondered if they'd be the last words I'd ever hear from the lady, thin as they come she was, frail if you can imagine a woman to be so who's still standing, begging for the life of her son to be spared, her own being discarded at the moment. Her face was pinched beyond recognition, and I would not know until later that I had known her almost 30 years earlier in Philadelphia, in another life.

"Dice often roll on the edges." I'd heard that someplace along the trail, back down yonder in Texas or Oklahoma in that other existence, me with a kid in my saddle lap, a kid who as yet had not spoken a word, had not said he missed his mother or father in a sick bed of sorts, or worse. The wind whipped itself into a new frenzy, sand and grit of all kinds and grass shreds coming first as thin as spider webs, touching at my eyelids, then the snow taking over, swirling sheets of it like linen frozen on a clothesline, John still not saying the first word. He was a lightweight four year old who wouldn't check out at more than 30 pounds. In a small way I warmed his body. In a way he warmed mine, but his heat different from my inner heat.

General, the horse I had ridden for three years, was working hard, now and then overcoming snow drifts formed the way the wind wanted them to be formed, and always against our progress. I could not see ten feet in front of me, cared now little for what was behind me. I had written them off, John's mother and father. I could almost hear the limbs breaking over their heads, crashing down heavy with snow and ice, smashing that little clumsy shelter to shreds, stealing from them their only chance at heat. If they survived the crash, the bears and wolves and peccaries would take over all remains. If the crashing produced bleeding, it would happen as soon as the storm was over.

It was getting colder, the snow heavier, the wind sharper, now and then wielding a sheer knife at the back of my neck, up my arms between gloves and sleeves, the worst kind of infiltrator, subtle at first but not secretive. I huddled John closer, felt him shivering, thought instantly of a fire, hoping wood was available, that Zac had been at his given work.

Then a series of doubts and questions began to rise up.

I could not afford to worry about my horse; if he didn't make it, we wouldn't. The mother and father back there in the makeshift cabin would last only as long as she could move, keep her mind, see the future coming. If she lost her husband, she'd have to roll him out of that little cabin; to stay with a dead man was somehow unthinkable, at least to me.

If we got into the canyon in decent shape, we had a good chance. The snow would be wind-swept and careen across the mountain top and passage through some of the canyons would be tolerable. In there, inside the canyons that ran in a hundred ways, firewood had been stored by miners who continually pawed through the area searching for gold. Only one rich find in about thirty years, but it had been a good one, and the dreamers kept coming. And old acquaintance Zac Olney, realizing his digging and clawing at mountain rock was useless for too long, had hauled wood for a few dollars a load. It was stuff he first just picked out of the timber lines, deadfalls, standing dead wood his horses could pull down. He hauled and dragged them into the canyons, the miners tossing a few bits onto his lap, sharing things at bartering. I'd seen a few of his firewood sites, tight and square under eaves of stone, under prominent cliff faces or in caves, stashed in some protective manner so rot wouldn't come before ignition. Later, seeing the profits of his labors, Zac began to tear down, rip out or up a mess of trees for half a dozen years, and then sawed, split, lugged and stashed the yield in many spots. Sometimes he had help. He got a second wagon. Sometimes the help stayed, sometimes not. Zac kept working and I depended on that determination of his.

As I rode, hugging John tighter, wondering how I found myself here, in this situation, I went back to the last town I'd been in. The cards fell in my favor there, my stake grew, and the ladies took a bit of it, as usual. I had too much tequila on the last night and left early in the morning, headed for Turpstown where my brother had a small ranch and needed help for the winter season. I had wondered off the trail looking for one of the water holes I knew had been still wet my last time through, not quite sure which canyon would take me right to it. When I came upon the little cabin some folk had built under some trees, three tree trunks being corner poles, and I knew they were not going to be there for the long stay, not for the whole winter that could pound at you like the ocean. Snow-heavy limbs would crash down on top of them and they'd be open to the worst of the winter beating across the plains and the edges of the mountains, sucking the heat right from their bodies.

I could not have painted it any worse than the way it hit me when I knocked on the real makeshift door.

I guessed, I saw, I smelled hopelessness, yet the woman offered me water and then a cup of coffee thinner than cow wire, haste boiled right into it.

The woman was frail as an old broom stick, her eyes sunken in her head, her hands shaking like leaves in the morning breeze. "My husband," she said in her very first words, "is sick and can't be moved. We have a bit of food, sufficient wood for fire, but little else besides frozen horsemeat." The kicker in their whole lot was a boy about 4 years old, a smiling tow head who had no idea of what was what. I knew her unsaid terror.

That was my introduction to the boy John, the 30-pounder now in my arms, still shivering. For the first time in more than half my lifetime, I was totally responsible for the safety and the life of a youngster. I had never wanted to be a father, now, for all practical purposes, I had a son. The thought and realization worked its way deep into me. I spoke to my horse; "C'mon, Gen'ral, show the troops what you're made of. Up an' at 'em, Gen'ral, time's awasting. Bless you, Gen'ral, and all that follow your line."

General broke another quickly-swirled bank of snow and plowed on. The heart of that great animal must have been heaving in that proud chest. Pride and sadness hit me at the same time, thinking about him; he had served me so well for those years and here I was putting him through another very difficult ordeal. I heard the wind break into a howl and knew its breath was being split by a canyon entrance, a fortunate sign. John nestled into my arms deeper as the snow and wind slammed against us, as the horse began to tire from his ordeal. I talked to him again. "We're closing in, Gen'ral, getting near some good cover. Won't be long now, big boy."

As always, I was being haunted, trying to put in place who I was. I admitted I was not immortal, not invincible, not sinless, and I could feel a ton of baggage hanging on my backside. It was then a series of doubts began their rise, crawling up my backside and becoming known. I asked questions. What if the wood was not there? What if Zac had been hurt and not able to complete his rounds? What if some raw-cold miner or prospector had seen the piles of wood and stole them for his own? What ifs grabbed me. The boy shivered more. The wind whistles and howls picked up, and suddenly in a matter of minutes it was as if we were in the eye of a storm center. The wind stopped careening across my face, stopped finding ways inside my clothes. The boy breathed loudly, like a gasp, like he knew what relief was like. We had turned into a canyon and found that relief. General felt it as much as we did; he plowed on a bit stronger.

In a deep refuge, sort of a cave within a cave, we found a pile of wood and a bundled pack of kindling knotted by a small length of rawhide under some stones on a ledge. An old sheet of canvas also lay bunched on the ledge with more rocks holding it down. I could picture it being stripped from a wagon broke down in the middle of the plains or against a river bank that had got in the way.

I was able to get General under decent cover and get some water into him from snow melt. The fire, meanwhile, was soon roaring, the heat touching us where needed, John sleeping soundly wrapped in a blanket and the old canvas likely left by Zac the savior. It was like heaven had come down out of the skies for us. From my pack I soon got the goods to get the coffee going and charred a bit of jerky for the smell of it, for the quick taste of it, and all other good memories.

We were not the first ones to find shelter here, and Zac surely had found this place. If I ever met him again, I'd treat him to a night at the nearest saloon. Zac was much of the goodness I had met in my time, a real piece of the land. I was feeling that life might not be so bad after all, after all I had been through, with Zac and others like him hanging in the mix of things, the country spreading farther west, getting as big as the mountains that often stood in the way of the westerly stuff. And the boy now becoming my full responsibility. I felt the weight of that responsibility as much as I felt the goodness setting in me about Zac, like opposite things always at work.

The coffee smell and the jerky stinging the air must have gone off on the quick wind and found a keen nose, or a hungry one. A voice came off a wall of the canyon like a gunshot. "Is that hot coffee I smell, stranger? Haven't had a mouth of it in three days."

I didn't know where he was except it wasn't far. "You a friendly sort, mister? If you are, you're welcome. Who are you?"

"Name's Tug Trubok. I been fiddlin' in the earth hereabouts and tryin' to hold out for the storm 'cause I wanted one more day of dreamin' 'fore I moved on. Plain got stuck and didn't dare head off in the storm to Newfield."

"Any hits? You got a good horse? C'mon over. Just follow your smeller. I have the coffee and some jerky burning itself ripe. You got anything to add, bring it."

In a matter of ten minutes Tug Trubok rode up to our place. We tied his horse up beside General who snorted a bit and welcomed the company.

Trubok said, "Here, I got some bear meat in a trade. Burn that ripe, if'n you can. See you found Zac's store of wood. Man's special, that's what he is. Came by about a month ago, three trips in a week or so settin' us up for winter. Said he was goin' to winter down in

10

Newfield 'til the fish was movin' again."

"Zac's an old friend of mine."

"Any friend of Zac's can move anywheres he wants hereabouts. Who's the boy? Your'n? Looks too tender for such weather. You just gettin' outta the storm?"

"I got him from his folks who have a mighty weak shed of a place back yonder. Looked to me, and his momma, that they wouldn't make it through the winter. Boy's father's sick as all get out. Boy's name is John Furlong."

Trubok set an inquisitive frown on his face, gulped a mouthful of coffee, and wiped his mustache and beard with the back of his hand. "Don't hear that name much out here." A nod, a cocking of his head, the set of his eyes, gave his next words extra attention. "Fact is I heard it in Newfield last visit. Man from Philadelphia, of all places back yonder, and he was lookin' for his brother havin' seen no hide nor hair of him in a passel of years since he left home."

"This Furlong drifting or looking?"

"Man's got his mind set on findin' his kin. Askin' questions all over, what I heard, kinda direct at it, like he's not gonna let go the reins no way. I heard him say any good word can be sent to him in Newfield or Coldville, either place any time 'cause someone there'll know where he's put himself."

I was really interested, thinking of the possibilities, the name, the errand I was on for the boy, the mission of this Furlong fellow. "So you saw this gent? Right in person? What sort of fellow is he? Make his way out here?" If he was the brother of the boy's father, I'd have my doubts about him, the shed he built for his family coming back into my mind, the poor frame of it, the horrible shortcuts at building.

I could have asked a hundred questions, even as the boy stirred in his sleep, rolled on one side, doubled up in decent comfort despite the weather. He was three feet from the fire, at the back end of the cave, and Trubok and I sat opposite each other, the fire between us.

Trubok nodded again. "Man's a sticker, I'll bet. Could work his way, but from what I heard won't have to. Comes from money back in Philadelphia, which means somethin' greased I'd guess, easy pullin's while he's on the search."

"Might have a connection here but I agree on the chances being slim. This country gets bigger every day, more people heading

11

here so all kinds of towns pop up to give them a place to set down. The boy's folks picked a bad spot out there in the far valley, lonely as a lobo on the prowl. I saw that right off, but we couldn't all make it out of that valley, partly heaven there and partly hell if you ask me. If you could bunk down there for the winter, be real comfortable, you'd probably love the place in spring. Some hard choices in between though."

"You gonna look up this Furlong fellow?"

"It's only honesty and promise kicking it in. Soon as we can get out of here, and get to Newfield, I'll do that right off. The boy'd have a chance if this gent's a relative and he's somewhat better at things than his father. "

We huddled in the caves for two days and the third day broke bright and clear and a good twenty degrees warmer, like spring might have a mind of sneaking up on us if we weren't holding the reins. In a full day's ride over wind-swept grass, now and then a snow drift built across the way, we got to Newfield. Lights were on in most of the buildings, the saloon, the small six-room hotel beside the saloon, a lantern in the livery where horses and men made comfortable noises at the end of day. All the while John sat quietly across the saddle like he was pocket change I was carrying. He hadn't even called for his mother yet. I was wondering if the boy could even talk.

Trubok and I made right for the saloon, after our horses were put up, to warm our bones, the boy's bones, to feel the sputter down the throat, the real welcome to a night of promised rest, and warmth. A piano was playing; the soft tinkles of the keys coming down the quiet street sounding like raindrops on a watering can. A girl's voice, like music itself, came to me as I carried the boy in my arms into the saloon.

Trubok headed right up the stairs to say hello to an old friend. I suspected that he'd have his drink upstairs, out of the way.

Every gent in the room looked up as I sat the boy on the bar and began rubbing his limbs. He still hadn't said a word. Not in all the ride had he said a word, nor in the caves those nights. And he had not cried either, not a whimper out of him, but I was sure he was a mute. A couple of gents nodded at me, one I had seen before, somewhere down the trail, and one who, I guessed, was saying his compliments on my bringing a young boy in out of the tough weather … though any one of them, I am sure, would have done the same

12

thing. Their interest did not flag as I kept rubbing him, and the barkeep set up a soft drink on the bar top.

I did notice that some of the older gents, who had worn their saddles to the nub, who had probably lost a son or two, in the war or on the plains spreading west, were taken with the image of the boy, the young, the new, the unspoiled future being seen now. A few of them walked by, patted the boy on his knee or me on the back and said nothing more than "howdy," and I knew the thrust of their simple message.

I admit a whole bunch of it got to me, finally realizing that I had saved his life for sure. I could picture the wreck of that shed that had been his short-time home, and the savage end that his parents might be having at the moment, or already had known. A three-day trip back into the remnants of the storm might find nothing, or find something. It hit me then that I'd have to go back. There was no other way.

A bang came from the door being slammed and another good looking gent came in and was talking to a few others who had been playing cards. His clothes were somewhat trail-worn, but I knew such duds had lots of service left in them, being well-made I could tell.

After ten minutes or so, me still rubbing the boy's limbs, him still quiet, no whining or whimpering, the stranger approached me and said, "You ought to get some food into that boy and a warm place to sleep. If you haven't got a place, you're welcome to my room right at the head of the stairs. I'll manage otherwise. They tell me you brought him in out of the storm. That's quite admirable of you, quite admirable, if I do say so."

"Mister," I said, "you say a lot of Philadelphia in your voice. You don't happen to go by the name of Furlong, do you? Don't tell me your name is Furlong. Don't tell me I'm that lucky."

"Mark Furlong it is, sir. I am all the way from Philadelphia, looking for my brother and his wife Enid who was a Paterville before she was married, of Brent Hall Patervilles. And what has luck to do with this and are you, sir, also Philadelphia born and bred? "

I almost fell on the floor. I had known her back in Brent Hall, as a young girl in the same end of town where I had grown up, to about the age of fifteen when I was out on the road in a huff, all in one day of misguided anger.

13

Now, I had withstood the ride with the boy and this latest surprise, both coming at me from out of nowhere. I was still in one piece, though not yet proof of anything from where I stood. Now I would see how well this other Philadelphian would handle his end of things.

"Mr. Furlong," I said, "I'd like you to meet your nephew, John Furlong." I put his hand on the boy's shoulder. I felt something I thought might have been energy, or something else I'd get a name for in a hurry.

But I think his mouth is still open.

"No way," Jed Lawson screamed, his voice full of hate and anger not heard in Tally's Pass all summer. He swung around at the bar and looked directly into the eyes of River Rowan as if either pair of eyes would ignite. "He ain't ours. He's mine. I raised him from the runty colt you wouldn't look at a second time. No way you claimin' him back from me."

He patted the gun at his hip. "Try it an' I'll kill you." The blue in his eyes was bright as a morning sky and they sat under shaggy brows in a sun-browned face the way most drovers looked after a drive.

"Hell, Jed, you ain't goin' to shoot me," Rowan said, "'cause my father'd chase you across Texas to kick your ass before he shot you good, and you know that."

Lawson stormed back at him. "You still ain't getting' my colt. He's the only thing I own right now since my pa died. I got nothin' to ride for 'cept that horse. I got nothin' else, no place to go, nothin' to grab, and you want to take my colt. It's been that way since you got the first choice at saddles your pa stuck in the barn. All them saddles was my father's. Every one of them, just like our place was until your pa stole it plain and simple."

"You keep sayin' that, Jed, an' I'll be the one doin' the killin', see if I don't." Rowan carried the same drover's looks that Lawson showed, like there were no other features acceptable in Tally's Pass or any Texas town.

At the end of the bar, Old Jack Scarborough, mountain denizen in town for another visit for good health, tired of the continuing threats at other's good health, popped up out of his seat and said, "That's not the colt we left with you boys! You boys was runnin' around shoutin' hell at each other all the time and none of you saw we had swapped one of our colts for yours. Him we got up in the hills, Lucifer's colt's now full growed and king of the hills."

Old Jack Scarborough said to Lawson, "Don't worry none, son. I pulled a switch on you. That's your colt we raised in the hills. We knowed you was runnin' against a stacked deck, losin' the ranch and all the gear and your daddy dyin' on top of it all, like goin' downhill he was for pretty near six months and had no fight left in him. That colt we consider yours, Jed, and his mommy, is still with

15

us, with me and Trighorn up there in the Skipper's End and he's got a whole herd of mares all to hisself right about now. And I can prove all this stuff I'm spittin' out."

"How?" Jed Lawson was so confused he didn't know what was going on. "How could I love my colt that ain't my colt and now's king of a herd of wild mares? How can I not know what's mine?"

Perplexity crossed Lawson's face that Scarborough could almost scrape off with his mountain knife. So much the young did not know, including these two young ones.

"Let the horses say so themselves," Scarborough said, "but let me tell you, we done a powerful good job raisin' him. Until he got loose with a filly one time but we had them locked into Skipper's End with no way out of that valley, and Lucifer Deuce, that's what we call him, kilt a cat up in there and stomped the hell out of him and we'd no idea there was dozens a horses locked in all the time just like they was corralled up regular like."

Scarborough swigged off the last of his drink and pointed at both Lawson and Rowan, winked at both of them in turn, turned a smile loose that was as mysterious coming from him like a big laugh in the middle of a stampede, and said, "You boys don't know nothin' like what me and Trighorn knows, about them horses and you boys. They been that way for months while you boys near a year been swappin' killin' talk and we know what you don't know ... that you're damned brothers, the pair of you. What say to that, huh?"

He waited for response and got none. "That get you kind of greasy in the saddle talkin' the way you do at each other? Like some chicken fat's been tossed up there on your saddle? Brothers, huh? Snake eyes, huh? Yoked, huh? An' how come? 'Cause you got the same momma, that's how come, but with different fathers and them boys as dumb as you two approachin' the same. Dang fools, whyn't you ever look in the mirror at the same time at each other? I thought all the time you was scairt to take that look, but now I see you're too dumb to. Whose eyes ain't your eyes but is? Can't you see your momma on the other side, kind of lookin' back at you? You're as smart about horses as about daddies, an' that ain't a helluva lot from where me and Trighorn been sittin' all this time."

Scarborough stepped away from the bar and said, "Course, you boys could come up into Skipper's End part of our world and

16

pay a visit, but don't come alone by yourself or we won't let you in and won't let you see Lucifer Deuce roamin' his own kingdom like he ought to cause me and Trighorn made him what he was born to be, like you boys should do your own same thing 'fore it's too late for either one of you, bein' brothers to start with."

He walked to the door and left and they could hear him as he mounted his horse and saying, "Best come like brothers, two at a time or don't come at all. I been too long at secrets I promised to keep in my shirt pocket long as I have and that lady of your mother was my sister and that makes me an uncle twice over. How's them for keepin' secrets f'ever almost."

The stunned silence in the room, the look in the mirror, the reflecting on the past rushed over them. The found brothers had a few drinks, made a pact, and went to visit their mother.

When the two of them walked into her kitchen, she was at the sink washing fruit, an apron in place, cleaned dinner dishes stacked up on a strainer at one end of the sink, the table cleared, and a look on her face that said she knew this day was coming.

She pointed at the table and bench and said, "Sit down. I knew this day would come and I always hoped it would be the two of you together and not one at a time. Thank you for that." A wisp of hair floated over one eye, which she brushed away with the back of her hand, and sat down at the table. She was a spry-looking woman in her early late thirties, mostly black hair with now-and-then gray flirting for entry, terribly blue eyes, a tanned face saying she did not spend her life in the kitchen, and a sense of command in her voice, as if she was used to difficult situations, or could see them coming from a distance, as though she had been there already, been there and come back.

Both sons thought it strange that she was showing some happiness at the moment there lives were in mass of chaos, duplicity, disbelief.

"This is how it happened," she said. "I was in love with your father, Jed, and we'd been fishing at the falls upriver and we made love on the most perfect of days in a joyous breeze. And I got pregnant. I was 16, but hid it pretty well. When my time came, he took me on a fishing trip and I had the baby in the hills and stayed with some of his friends and came back, but he kept you with him, Jed, and seemed to drift away right after that. I thought he was gone forever, and I went out with your father, River, and we got married and we had you, and I looked up one day when you were about two and I saw your brother in Haggerty's Store for the first time."

She released a smile as broad as dawn. "The minute I saw you, Jed, I knew who you were, and then I saw your father, and he put a shushing finger to his lips and we had our secret and he never said a word about it to me or anybody else for all these years because he knew what it would be like for me, living here. Tally's Pass is a lot different from what you think. It has some deepness that's hard to understand at times, like a balky horse you're not sure what's going on with it, or what it's going to do. I was never in a position to change that. I'm still not, but now I know I'll fight it and your father, River, will never be mad at me, thank goodness for that. He is a fine man and I love him."

Her smile was radiant as she said, "Both of them were grand to me, and grand to you if you think about it. You grew so well, both of you. I saw a lot of you, Jed, because your father bought the small spread to be near, but the trouble started back a few years. I don't know how it started, but land grabs some men like they're grabbing their women from trouble, trying to protect, cover over, thinking they own it outright."

Once, in the midst of some thought, she looked out the window at the grass running for miles, in the distance the mountains touching the sky. Each of her sons saw memories moving in the stillness of that look.

"They were both good men," she vouched. "One never told and one never suspected what I had done. It doesn't get any better than that for a young girl who grows up with two children, one she hugs all the time and one she misses hugging all the time. It was not easy, but I could never cry or scream or let go, because it would all be over in a flash of something I dared not bring about. It was living two lives at once, one here with you, River, and one there where you were, Jed, so near and so far. And two men to keep comfortable. Being as hard as anything you can imagine, one here with me and one not, just like the two of you. Just think about how much you have shared without knowing a word about it."

The look of being chewed up by memories, or finding some solace in them, came back on her. "When I heard about the trouble with the colt, Lucifer's colt, I told Jack Scarborough about it and he

18

and his pard Trighorn planned the whole thing. That was another secret weighing on me, but tolerable as long as there were no fisticuffs. I swear I'd come apart at that, you boys fighting. Your fathers had arguments, plenty of them at the end, Jed, when he was trying to save something for you, and he knew he couldn't do it. We talked once at the river, the first time in years, and he swore he'd never tell on me, even knowing it would hurt you, Jed, and you too, River."

She looked away again and said, "So I was lucky and unlucky at the same time, Happy and unhappy, as you can imagine. Loved two ways by two men. A whole mess of a life in two parts, as if I had been set apart by a butcher with a keen knife. But I'd do it all again for the two of you." Her hands stretched across the kitchen table and the grasp she had dreamed about came to her, and the two brothers silently shook hands under the table.

She only sensed it happening at first, but knew it did.

"Tomorrow, if you've a mind," she said, "and River's father is okay with it, which I am sure he will be, we can all take a ride up there at Skipper's End to see Lucifer Deuce. Jack told me he is one magnificent animal."

What her face was saying to the two of them was that which had drifted apart had drifted back together again.

Red Cornell came up out of Grace Canyon into bright sunlight, a small breeze under his hat brim and across his face, and a spread of yellow flowers out on the grass as far as he could see. Not a living thing brought any movement to his eyes, except for a large-winged bird sitting on a shelf of air high over his head. "Stillness can be smothering, Chaps," he said to his horse riding under him smooth as ever. "We've been sitting still too long, old boy, waiting for those rustlers to make a move."

In that stillness he saw a momentary reflection, looked again, and could not find it. "An empty bottle," he said to Chaps, "or a piece of a busted bottle some cowpoke tossed aside, the sun working on it now."

Cornell, ramrod straight in the saddle, was almost as broad across the shoulders as his favored mount, and a barrel chest aside a rugged pair of arms. On his head, trailing a drawstring under his chin, the once-white Stetson had changed color, advancing into a faded yellow with one bullet hole in the brim and months of trail dust settled into the fabric. The faded blue shirt and vest, as well as the dark denim pants, showed off his past week's work alone at the foothills of Waller's Mountain and the endless chain of caves, canyons, wallows, and deep recesses leading in places toward the heart of the mountain itself. He'd been over more than three quarters of Waller's Mountain and the rest of the nearby chain where he could ride without so much as a scent of rustled beeves. Some days, like today he could have said, lie as still as the hour just before dawn when it begins to shake the world awake.

Cornell had been through a tough stretch in a week's time; his boss's herd hit by rustlers, three or four hundred head run off, one wrangler shot in the shoulder, the trail of the rustled cows disappeared at the river's edge, and Cornell ordered to go out alone to see what he could find, "No matter how long it takes, Red," the boss, Colonel Slats Merrison said, blessing the commission. "I want those rustlers more than I want those cows back. It might save us some work down the trail." He added, with a smile, "Course, I'd like to see us get those cows back too."

Cornell, coming out of the canyon, showed much of his wild red hair, nearly a bushel of it. It sat down on the back of his neck like a flag, crowded out of his hat atop his ears, and most likely filled the peak of his hat. The dense redness found a matching acceptance in the intense, deep blue of his eyes that had few parallels in sighting a target. It was the first thing the Colonel looked for in a new hand, a steady hand with a steady and unblinking eye when trouble came, as it usually did in any part of any month, and any place cows where were gathered or pushed apart.

"I tell you this, men," he'd say to new hires, "there are men out there who want to reap the profits on your hard work. They want to take your share out of your hands in one sneaky maneuver and run off with all they can. Don't let them take your share, or, by God, my share." It drew in the ranks for the old Shilo legend, the straightest man Cornell ever met. And the Colonel, long in cavalry command, found Cornell to be a man exceeding his demand for trust, good sense and old-style cavalry skills. What he guessed stood out as another quality was an instinct that Cornell himself felt controlled his actions at certain times.

That instinct called a halt to his movements in the foothills of Waller's Mountain, when for the third time he saw the reflection coming at him off the grass, though he was now in an entirely different position. The singular reflection came again from out there on the wide prairie, amid the flowers going crazy and the sun slanting onto a special surface. He almost heard it say, "Whoa," much as he would say to Chaps on the move.

The third time he saw the reflection made his second sense work for the first time in the new day. The reins flipped over in his hand and Chaps headed downhill, straight for the spot that Cornell had marked by crossed lines in two directions, on two peaks and a lone tree and a significant outcrop on a slow rise. As he rode, intent on keeping true his sighting line, he thought of some fabulous find coming his way, a key to the mystery of the stolen cows and their current location.

The reflections turned out to be from a broken spur, with a bit of silver on it, sitting face up on a bare piece of ground. Cornell stared down at it, was about to ride away, and heard the voice say again, "Whoa, Cornell. Whoa." He dismounted, picked up the spur and stuck it in his saddle bag. This he did because he believed something in the day would tell him why he had picked up a broken spur.

21

For the moment he rode on, oblivious of the impact that spur would have, and what the Colonel would have to say later.

Back up into the foothills he guided Chaps as his search went on and yielded nothing for hours. If despair had its way with him, he would have chucked it on one harsh climb, but Chaps was also equal to the task, though the search continued fruitless, the climbs at times rugged and awkward.

On one sharp turn in the trail, the tree line behind him, a hawk careening across the skies and letting go a shriek, Chaps reacted to the sound and Cornell felt a pinch of sense, like that belonging to the everlasting partnership of horse and rider. And at that precise moment, as if through an open window, he saw himself checking out a source back in town, looking for an answer to a question that came on him with a subtle intrusion.

The whole town scene shaped up in his mind; no names, no faces, but as actual as it could be.

"C'mon, Chaps," he said, "let's go back to town and look for a few answers. We got nothing out here."

Late in the day, the sun an orange blob getting cut in half by a distant mountain plateau, Cornell left his horse at the livery and walked the boardwalk toward the Fremont City Saloon. Late afternoon dropped its veil atop the saloon, and cards sent out their slap and shuffle sounds, glasses tinkled and tinkered with day's end, and a cloud of cigar smoke slipped out the door to lose itself in evening's grasp.

Reasons for all his actions mounted in summary for Cornell; the sun had reflected off the broken spur not once, not twice, but three times, for a reason. He had picked up the spur, for a reason. He had come back into town, for a reason. And he kept trying to find his way through those essential arguments.

In the saloon, standing at the bar having a beer, an old image came back to him; he had seen spurs like the broken one before ... and in this room. He looked around the whole saloon, at the spread of boots on a host of cowpokes and did not find any resolution for his search. There were no exact matches to his find out on the prairie. The fact bothered him, for there were many kinds of spurs on the boots of cowpokes in the mix of jobs, errands, and come-and-go visits.

But he was not bewildered. The vision he had seen out there

22

while he was on the hillside came back to him in a flash and he left his beer on the saloon bar and went straight to the general store.

Dace Harkins, the storekeeper, sat on his stool in the store, chewing the remains of an apple. The odor, fresh as morning dew, cut through the atmosphere of the store as Cornell pulled the broken spur from his vest pocket and placed it on the counter.

"Dace," he said, asserting a bit of secrecy in his approach, his voice just above a whisper, a wary look back over his shoulder, "do you carry this kind of spur in the store? Just like this one? I'd like to know for a personal reason." Harkins had been around in the business a long time and Cornell figured he'd never let a customer's secret out of the bag, if he could help it.

"Sure do, Red. I've had that brand here for a while. In fact I sold a set to a gent just a few days ago. Said he broke his in a rockslide in the hills. Sounded lucky to me, just losing a spur."

"Are they really special, Dace? Nobody out our way uses them. They fairly new, are they?"

"Far as I know, they are, Red. That fella, Winchell, started working the Box Bar spread a while back, and said he favored them since his brother bought him his first pair over in California last year, with some silver inlaid on them. They're called the Sonora-style. Winchell, he's the fella broke one and then lost it, is a big guy with a white beard about a foot long I'd bet." He set his hand across the middle of his chest. "All the way down to here. Now and then wears some of his dinner in it." He laughed a half laugh and looked around to make sure nobody else was in hearing distance. "I wouldn't lie, no way."

Twisting his head to an inquisitive angle, lowering his voice, Harkins said, "Where'd you come across this one, Red? You been up there in the rocks? Or are you onto something maybe I might guess at?" Now he had a half smile, like he was saying, "It's all safe with me."

Cornell did not like the look, or the half smile, so he laid things on the line for the storekeeper. "You say one word to anybody, even your wife, about this little talk we're having, and you'll find yourself a hell of a lot sorrier than you are now, if I make myself clear." He put a hard finger onto Harkins' chest, and tapped him a couple of times. "Real sorry, just about as sorry as I can make it."

23

Red Cornell, big and mean all over, walked out of the store, looked back in and pointed one more time at Harkins, who was still holding his breath, and headed for the saloon.

As the evening closed down in the saloon, a few stray customers in and out at the late hours, Cornell spotted the long white beard on a big man coming in and stepping to the bar. Dropping a coin on the bar, the bearded cowpoke said, "Whiskey, Slate," to the bartender, "I have to get back to the spread."

The bartender said, "You'll get there in time for breakfast, big boy."

Cornell, leaving without much notice at all, sat on his horse a few minutes later outside town. Shortly he heard the hoof beats of a horse and saw the shadow of the big man riding out, not toward the Box Bar spread, but toward Waller's Mountain and its looming darkness out on the horizon.

His instincts, he believed, had kicked in on a decent start.

Cornell set himself well back of Winchell who rode straight toward the hills, paying little attention to the trail behind him. And Cornell knew he could always follow Winchell's tracks, if need be, come daylight, for his direction was dead straight to one point in Waller's Mountain, as far away from Grace Canyon as could be. Cornell, wishing he knew the area better, rode Chaps at a slow pace, trying to keep his own shadow off the skyline, favoring lower tracks in the landscape whenever possible. He felt as if he was on a scouting mission back in the war.

Winchell, heedless of the man tracking him, headed right to a certain spot of the mountain face and disappeared as if swallowed up, a shadow going into shadows as far as Cornell was concerned. The slim entrance, on foot exploration by the big redhead, led into a canyon that spread-eagled once inside that slight passage. Cornell agreed that it looked like a holding pen. On foot, still on a mission as commanded, Cornell explored the whole layout of the little valley hideaway after he placed his spurs in his saddlebag; there was grass, there was water, there was a cave where the embers of a late fire glowed in the darkness. The rustled cattle, content with grass and water, idled quietly and at ease, as one man on guard made a leisurely ride back and forth across the slim entrance.

In the morning, with the sun behind him, Cornell rode up to the Colonel at the ranch house.

"How'd it go, Red? You see anything out there?" Merrison, the good judge of men, sat on his porch smoking a pipe, expectancy sitting in his face.

"I found the cows, Colonel. There's about 400 of them in a small canyon way at the other end of the mountain, and well across the river."

"How many men?"

"Only five of them, Colonel. And they're getting some more cows from up that end of the range. I heard them talking last night. They're pretty jittery, if I'm a judge of things. They want to get it done and get out from under."

"How shall we handle it, Red? I'm taking your play on it."

"I thought about that all during my ride back here, Colonel. We got them penned up right now, like they were in prison already. We can bring judge and jury with us and hold the trial right on the spot. The cattle in there are yours, every last one of them as far as I'm concerned. We could get in and get behind them, scatter the herd. Those boys would be all over themselves trying to get out of the way, but they'd only get crimped up by that narrow passage." He added, after further thought, "I can get us in, all of us. Then we sit them down and hold court and all the evidence would be right in front of us. That'd wrap things up, Colonel."

"Be damned if that ain't a good idea," Merrison exclaimed, a full smile crowding his face, with the promise of justice looming as a positive outcome. He kept nodding, kept finding affirmation in his judgment of men, even as he had questions that piqued his curiosity. "How'd you find them, Red? "

The bushy-haired red head, smiling all the while as if a secret would never be revealed, said, "I just kind of reflected on things, Colonel, and after that it was a piece of cake, as they say."

A Saddle in the Desert

He was in the sparse land between shifting sands of the great desert and the last tree bearing green when he saw the vultures descending from their high flight. Breward Chandler, "Brew" to friends back in the mountains where breathing was much easier than here in the midst of little life, sat bareback on an Indian pony he had freed from a natural corral behind a blow-down. Chandler had learned that the horse would obey pulls on his mane and in this manner he had escaped from sure capture by heading into the desert, with his pistols loaded and a lariat and a canteen he had grabbed on the run. He was not sure who was after him, either renegade Indians or renegade whites out for the kill, looking for guns, clothes, saddles, anything for free. He was hoping that they'd measure the little he might have against the rigors of a chase in the desert. Perhaps, he also hoped, they were smarter than he thought they were.

The canteen was almost empty and water had to be found.

Now, arrowed out of the high sky, he saw the vultures drop down and out of sight ahead of him. There was no hesitation on his part; he'd have to check the attraction. It might only be a natural desert kill, but it could be a man caught in the last tremors of life and death, a man like him, on the run from one thing or another. It was easy to see that life was full of such chases; he was proof of it.

He dipped into a slight swale, crested a small hill as much dune as he had imagined, and saw the horde of black birds at the carcass of a horse, the saddle in place. Chandler, watching them feast on the horse's flesh, stayed in place, now and then looking back over his shoulder for signs of any pursuit.

In less than half an hour the vultures had almost stripped the bones of flesh. Hoping they had done little damage to the saddle, he galloped in on the hungry critters and drove them off. Shortly they were aligned again high overhead on the lift of a thermal, like people waiting to get into church or for a general store to open its doors.

To his everlasting thanks, the saddle was undamaged and did not take him long to get it off the carcass remnants and onto the pony. The pony, not surprising Chandler, did not like the smell of death that came upon him, but he held the pony in place by hobbling his front legs.

The saddle looked to be a good old Texas saddle, with a high

26

back, one that would have lasted the rider for life, wherever he was. Or if he was. The initials LGT were burned into the pommel textured into the skirts, and the whole rig showed a few years of use. He'd have to look for the owner, see if he had fallen off, had been wounded, died of thirst. He could not tell how the horse had died. He assumed that if the rider was dead out there somewhere the vultures would have gone after him also.

Chandler only agreed that he would search ahead of him on the trail for the owner, not behind him, not wanting to run into those chasing him, or had been chasing him. The desert, he wished again, might hold them back.

When he rode off, sitting comfortable at last on the pony, the vultures returned to their feeding, and no signs of pursuit appeared on the wide horizon. Chandler figured his pursuers had backed off because of the desert threats. Ahead of him, near the Barracks Rim, sat a waterhole the old Kiowa, Bent Wing, had told him about earlier in time, the night they had sat outside Knock's Tavern at the junction of three trails in the mountains. Knock himself had introduced Chandler to Bent Wing, saying, "Listen to all he says, son. He knows more than any ten mountain men I know. He knows mountain and desert, grass and foothills, forest and canyon, like no one else does. And it's all free for you. I saved his life one time and he ain't never forgot it. No sir, not Bent Wing, Kiowa of all Kiowas. You mark every word he says. And he says things that will matter to you sometime down the trail, where things happen to a man the way they have for a thousand years out here, and he knows it all. Count on it. Came down to him from all the shamans that come before him, loading him up."

Knock had shaken his finger right in Chandler's nose at the end of that discussion; "Don't think him an old Indian blowing steam, boy. Just realize what he says will save your life someday. He ain't talking for nothing, he's talking good 'cause he's still trying to pay me back, being good to friends of mine."

Through Chandler's mind went the location of half a dozen waterholes in the range of the desert. The markers came back to him from his lessons at the tent of the Kiowa that one night outside Knock's Tavern. "One water hole is like a breath of air in the desert, and sits near the Barracks Rim where the old fort used to be. The elder of all shamans told me it runs a thousand feet underground to

27

cleanse itself for thirsty men. Comes clear through the mountain from a high lake the great god made."

Bent Wing told him about more water holes the Kiowa gods had sent to his tribe. "We share what has been given to us. You must do the same."

"Have any of them gone dry?"

"Oh, many. Those that were hidden from a decent thirst were fired dry by an angry god. No man owns a water hole."

Land marks had been explained to him by Bent Wing, places to look for, to look from, measures to be made, marks that were left for Indian eyes now coming to his eyes. The eagle talon on the face of a rock as he closed on Barracks Rim told him the waterhole was close enough to grasp. He found the slit of water at the base of Barracks Rim, in a cluster of rocks. In half an hour he had filled his canteen. The water had appeared in a slit of rock and disappeared in the rock cluster not pooling up at all. He had never seen one like it, and was thankful the old Kiowa had shared its location with him.

As Chandler prepared to leave he caught sight of a flash of sunlight reflected from a surface down the trail ahead of him. It flashed again and then it flashed again. A minute later it flashed again.

Someone was signaling him. Chandler looked down at the initials on the saddle, thinking he had found the saddle owner, that he had found LGT.

Chandler urged the pony toward the flashing source, perhaps a mile away. Behind him there appeared to be no pursuit, and under him the saddle, LGT's saddle, was new to him but comfortable in a few strides of the Indian pony. With nothing behind him, Chandler wondered what was in front of him. Would he find LGT up there with the reflections, obvious signals for help? If it was the owner of the saddle, he'd be riding bareback again. Perhaps soon.

Perhaps not. The place of the signals he had marked by an overhanging outcrop, a bulge that Bent Wing would have attributed to the Great God pushing on the earth, making new places, new gardens, new forests, and, of course, to test man, new deserts.

From a hundred feet away he saw the man's arm swing slowly, the way a tired man swings his arm or a wounded man. Chandler, approaching with caution, knew from about ten feet that the man was wounded. Blood was all over his shirt, one arm solely red. It was not

28

the arm he had waved.

"I'm glad to see you, mister. I thought I'd never get another drink of water. I'm bone dry, near dead, but want a drink of water." Then, after looking at the pony, he said, "I see you found my saddle."

"You LGT?"

With his finger pointing at Chandler's canteen, he said, "Yes, Lorne Taylor. I'm from the Barrel Ranch, the Bar-Circle-B. Got jumped by some renegades and galloped down this way hoping they wouldn't chase me. But a round caught me square from a long way off and I crawled in here as my horse ran off. Must have been hit too."

"What's the G for?"

"Gawaian. My father brought it from Australia a long time ago. It's a native name, like he wanted to hold onto something. He jumped ship on the west coast. Was a sailor and became a herder. Had enough of the sea."

Chandler held the canteen as Taylor took a small sip, then a gulp. "Sorry for taking your water, but it's a swap ... you got my saddle." He tried to laugh, but it didn't come out right. He coughed deeply.

"My pals will be looking for me," he said. "If they find you with my saddle you better be able to explain in a hurry why you have it. I can't be any clearer than that. They'll look for me until they find me, no matter what shape I'm in."

He coughed again, and this time it was deep and sounded as if it was not going to let go of him.

He waited until he caught his breath, and Chandler knew he was in the presence of a tough, tough man, who said, "If I had a pencil and paper I'd write you a bill of sale, my saddle for the best drink of water I ever had, but I haven't got them. If they catch up to you tell them my middle name. That'll be proof enough that I gave it to you. I won't make it out of here, I know that. Tell them my last thoughts find them doing what they like best. You have to swear to that."

"I swear," Chandler said. "I swear." He raised his hand.

Taylor began a small litany. "One's a singer and writes his own songs, plays great guitar. One would rather fish than anything in the world and then eat the catch at an open fire. He's a dreamer, but a worker like the others. One's a lover, enough said. But they're all

29

good men on a drive. We've been together for a long time. Since we were half a knee high. Be careful, though; they can be impulsive when one of us has been hurt or misjudged or even called a bad name out of turn, the likes of which have started a minor brawl or two in a few saloons."

Besides the coughing, Chandler knew other things were working down in Taylor. His face grimaced several times, the way one might measure the onslaught of different pains, how deep they went, how long they lasted.

"What are their names?" Chandler said.

Taylor, about to speak, held one hand up in a pause, took a noisy, deep breath, shook, looked at Chandler right in the eyes, and died on the spot. Blood ran from his mouth in one gush, and stopped, as if the whole mechanism of the body quit on the spot after a final shiver and shake that ran down his frame.

Always looking around him for signs of danger, checking out every swirl of dust, Chandler assembled enough rocks and stones and limestone slabs at the foot of the rim to inter LG Taylor from the ravages of animals and vultures. The only mark he left was scratched into the face of the cliff … LGT. A good eye would be able to see the letters.

Taylor's hat, a good Stetson, became Chandler's, but he left Taylor's boots in place, burying them with the man under the pile of rocks. He did not want to step into the other man's boots, plain and simple. The Good Words were spoken over the site and Chandler, with renewed spirit, set off again.

Late in the day, after drifting across an arid stretch of land, he found a break in the cliff face and started the climb to the top of Barracks Rim. At the top, after an arduous trip even for the Indian pony, he was in an instant surrounded by five riders.

"We heard you coming up, mister, so we just waited." The speaker not only sounded mean, he looked mean, as he said, "Tell me where you got that saddle, mister. And you better be clean and quick about it." His hands bore two Smith & Wesson shooters, aimed right at Chandler. "Say it all slow, mister, but say it all."

"The saddle was given to me by a man named Lorne Taylor. I found him wounded down below the rim. He said he was chased by some renegades though he wasn't sure if they were Indians or what. I think it might have been the same ones who chased me, got my horse."

"Where'd you get the pony?"

"He was trapped in the corner of a canyon by a blow-down that cut his escape route. I had to break his way out of there. Those who were chasing me went right past the blow-down and the pony kept quiet. But they might still be after me."

"So where's this Taylor fella you're talking about?"

"I buried him down below the rim. Marked the wall with his initials, like on his saddle. See, LGT there." He pointed down at the skirt of the saddle.

"Maybe you killed him. How does that sound? How do we know you ain't lying about it all? Even making up the story about him giving you his saddle. Where's his horse?"

"Gone to vulture food," Chandler replied. "I saw it straight off. They dropped in on the horse like they were shot at it. Half the animal gone when I came close on them."

"Where was the rider?"

"I got the saddle off and put it on the pony and a bit later I saw some flashing from the base of the rim. That's where I found Taylor, been shot bad. Said he'd write me a bill of sale for the saddle, but had no pencil."

The reply was still mean. "You could have made it all this up."

"Told me his pards would come. Told me about them. The singer. The lover. The fisherman. That you boys?"

"You could have heard that from anybody who knows us. None of it is secret. We don't know if we'll believe you or not. You got his hat." He looked down at Chandler's boots after he checked the Stetson. "Where's his boots?"

"On him when I buried him. I didn't need them, but I didn't have a hat."

"Anything else?"

"Told me what "G" stands for."

"Oh, yah, what for?"

"Said his daddy brought it all the way from Australia when he jumped ship on the coast. Stands for Gawaian, some native name."

"That's okay with us then. You sound like you treated Lorne square. Let's see where you buried him. We have to say our words for him. He was a good cowpoke, a good friend to all of us. We'll

31

miss him. We'll miss him a lot."

He shifted in the saddle, looked at his pals and said, "Let's take care of this and then tomorrow we'll chase down those coyotes. We'll need a horse for this fella. What's your name, mister?"

"Breward Chandler. No middle initial. They call me Brew. I was on my way to a new job in Parkersville."

"For now, Brew, you got another new job."

They all started back down the trail, through the break in the rim, with Chandler in the lead. They were just about at the bottom when he threw up his hand after he had spotted movement back along the base of the cliff. It was not more vultures but half a dozen riders just about where he had covered Taylor with rocks.

One by one the new friendship team slipped into a low break in the land, and moved half way to the group of men working at the burial site.

They were disinterring LG Taylor.

Without a signal of any kind, like a single mind was working, the men charged at the men at the site. The battle did not last long. And one man lived long enough to tell them who he and his pards worked for, and why.

Chandler, as it turned out, was no longer just along for the ride … he had become one of them, and sat the saddle that had always had been part of them.

To a man, Chandler knew, they would see justice was done, to one and all.

Clutch Maynard, still saddle-worthy though he had too much to drink, heard the music coming from Saddler's barn, where the dance bounced against the walls, shaking Wells' Ford to the joists. The fiddles, enough for an army, set his feet moving in the stirrups in an odd rhythm. He didn't care how drunk he might be, he was going dancing. "A bit of dancin' s what I need now," he said, knowing his horse understood every word out of his mouth. "I been too far, Big Jack, doin' too much, seein' one side of hell, not to have a piece of music for my own, slow down and lazy like I'm hearin' right now."

The buzz in his head was telling him to hold his mouth when he got inside. No need to let the whole town hear what happened.

They'd know soon enough, what he had come across, what had happened at the Bar J. He'd get JJ Johnson aside and tell him, away from his wife and other people just bent on dancing, having a high old time of it.

On the way home to Wells Ford from a long trail drive clear up the Masterson Trail, the sour smell of something burning beside wood had come down the draw on a slight breeze. Burnt leather might be in the smell, and hair of one kind or another. Big Jack gave him first notice, snickering, jerking his head on the reins, holding back a step in his pace like he would if a rattler lay in ambush. The odor turned riper in a hurry and when he climbed out of the draw he saw the smoke twirling in the air above the Bar J spread. The ranch house and the bunkhouse were not yet in sight, but the climbing smoke sank down into his gut. He spurred Big Jack toward the ranch.

He searched and found no bodies in the front of the house, while the back part was still smoldering. The huge brick wall and fireplace had kept the fire in the back of the house, but the barn was gone and the horses turned out. They grazed in a far field, under a tree. The thoughts he entertained tried to stick in his mind, but he lost them.

He did not see one head of beef on the whole place. Or anybody moving about the way they would normally be moving with a rider coming in, even straight off the grass.

A ranch hand, one he'd known simply as Dusty, lay shot dead in the back of the barn. The bullet had gotten him in the back of the head; bushwhacked. Maynard figured whoever had done the deed had snuck up that way, by the rear of the barn where the trees clustered against the wind.

He put the fire out that was trickling yet at the rear of the house and buried Dusty, before buzzards, sitting up there on thermals as if they were held up by strings, dropped in to tear him apart. The thoughts of such desecration made him shiver, as every cowman he knew dreaded being torn apart by the buzzards as the worst of death, worse than Hell itself making way for them.

Then, studying the kitchen, his eye seeing things that were set in the usual way in the Bar J kitchen, he spotted leavings that were not so usual. "Remember what you have seen" were words that, in his haste to get humane tasks under way and completed, filtered into his mind and floated around in the fog those words had encountered.

Maynard, believing all tasks completed, yet shaken and thirsty from his long ride, grabbed a bottle he knew was tucked under the pump housing at the sink. He set out to get himself drunk, getting the job done before he got to town, heard the music coming strong from Saddler's barn.

How would he tell JJ his barn and half the house were gone, and Dusty killed, put down now for eternal protection?

Whoever it was that bushwhacked Dusty, was a lefty, he said to himself, as if trying to put the fact in place to be remembered, to be remembered for a long time. His stomach rolled again as he thought about Dusty being dropped with one shot and left on the ground where he fell, left for the buzzards or the peccaries if they smelled his blood, if they dared come near fire.

Big Jack slowed at the Saddler's barn and stepped up to a spot at a tie rail as the fiddles twanged away at an old favorite Maynard's, "Sarah of the Seven Hills." A hundred times on the trail he had pictured Sarah coming into town, as he hummed the song. Wouldn't it be something if Sarah was waiting inside for him and not JJ, not a guy whose barn was gone and half his house, and a ranch hand shot dead in the back and now in the ground, killed by what? By who? He snapped his head about trying to remember what he was supposed to remember. Wasn't there something he had to remember, something to tell JJ? Something to tell the sheriff when he saw him? Maynard, tottering on his feet, his legs aching from his toes to his thighs, shook his head again, foggy at best.

Big Jack stopped in place at the rail and Maynard slid clumsily

34

off the saddle. His legs hurt, his backside hurt, his gut was burning, and his ears buzzing. The buzz came again the way it had been coming since he had left the Bar J, a long, moaning buzz. Now the fiddles were playing along with the buzz or playing him along. The empty bottle was tossed aside. It had been empty for half the ride.

He straightened his knees as he had done every time coming off the saddle after a long, hard ride. In his boots all ten toes ached to be free. The bottle did not take away much of his pain. Tipsy or not, this was going to be a tough one. And he hoped all JJ's family had come to the dance … he was sure there were no other bodies at the ranch. The rooms left standing were empty; he had double-checked. Sarah slammed into his mind again as he leaned on the door. Now his mouth must be still; say nothing, do nothing, until he had taken JJ aside. Get him alone. Be smooth about it. Ask first after the family.

Maynard leaned on the door, pushed it open, and fell into the barn directly onto the floor full of folks dancing like it was shivaree. The floor came up to meet his face. The floor was black as soot and so loomed his mind. The music must have stopped.

Maynard, his throat burning, his head still buzzing, woke up sitting up against a wall. JJ and the sheriff were standing over him, asking questions, making comments.

"Wonder what old Clutch was up to now." The sheriff looked around the roomful of folks looking on. "Wasn't Clutch on a drive with Masterson? Who saw him last?"

"One cowpoke answered from the crowd. "Saw him not more than two months ago, day he left with Jake and Henry Sills, heading out with young Masterson the day the drive was to start."

"Well," JJ said, "he got hold of a bottle to get him home. Was likely looking to celebrate the end of the drive."

JJ's voice dipped deep into Maynard's consciousness. He had worked for JJ on several jobs, including trail work. The voice made his head spin. He couldn't hold back. "Someone burned half your place, JJ. I smelled the smoke from way back in the big draw, first smelled like leather was burning. The whole barn is gone, roof timbers smoking on the ground and the back half the house. Dusty was bushwhacked, shot in the back of the head. I buried him between the barn and the first tree. Smack in the middle between them. He was awful bloody. I worried about the critters." Looking around for familiar faces, he said, "Is all your family here? The horses must

35

have been turned out before the fire was started. They were grazing by the tree line. No cows in sight, though." He asked again, "Is all your family here?"

JJ was upright directly in front of him. Tall, broad and fair, he had been a good boss to work for. He was a man with two feet on the ground when he wasn't on a horse. "They're all here, Clutch, the whole family. Thanks for asking. You see anybody? All the horses out okay? All the cows gone? Any sign around?"

From the side of the barn another voice yelled out, "Let's go get 'em, JJ, whoever pulled this stunt. Let's get 'em and hang 'em where it hurts."

Maynard shook his head and replied, "I'm supposed to remember something, JJ, but I can't find it." As if angry with himself, he shook his head again. "It's about your kitchen, JJ. Something in your kitchen. I looked to see if there was anybody dead besides Dusty. I was afraid of what I'd find. But nobody was there. At least, no one dead there. I don't know about the barn. It was still smoky, but no flames. I couldn't have helped anybody was still in the barn. I thought about the kids."

In a knee-jerk reaction, JJ scanned the crowd, marked faces of his family, and said, "They're all here, Clutch. Thanks for thinking about them. You have a good eye, I remember. So I won't sweat you forgetting. It'll come back. We came in last night. Mame and I spent the night at the hotel and the kids with Aunt Bessie. When do you figure it all started? Any sign of that? Nobody past us out there but the mountains and those canyons not much use to any of us."

Maynard's head still buzzed and the fuzziness seemed rounded up in a dark shadow. He tried to see all the scenes in his mind, but clutter came on his thinking; Dusty there behind the barn down and bloody, smell of leather burning, smoke rising into the sky like Indian signals and the awful silence that comes with death.

It all made him shiver but again with effort he tried thinking past the images in his mind. His voice came back clearer than it had been a second before, JJ staring at him like he was priming the pump in the kitchen, thirsty but patient.

"Had to be late yesterday, JJ, after you left for town. Dusty was behind the barn when he was shot. Must have still been daylight, though. Maybe he went out to check on something going on, some noise or ruckus out back there. He had no lantern with him."

36

JJ offered, "Dusty was a good old boy. Been with me a long time. I'll have to let his brother know. He's over in Mesa Verdi with Dutch Fallon's crew. Been there f'ever, like Dusty. Names Oliver."

"What's their last name?" Maynard said.

"Twitchell," JJ replied, "Stanley and Oliver Twitchell, come down from Oregon country way back when forever started it seems. Good boys all around."

One cowpoke, the same one who wanted to "get 'em and hang 'em where it hurts," stepped out of the crowd. "C'mon, JJ, let's posse up and chase hell outta them critters that done this."

Maynard recognized the impatient cowpoke as a lazy burn, a smoldering man who did little to add to his place in life, hanging around where he could pick up easy goods, working when he only had to get a meal or buy a bottle or pay a debt. The poke's name came in a rush – Toss Margins.

"No rushing around like chickens near a coyote," JJ said.

"Why not?" Margins replied, edging his way closer.

Maynard looked up at Margins, felt the "shiftlessness" coming right off the man's skin, and the phony demands in his words and in his voice, like he didn't mean what he was saying. And he focused his eyes on Margins, how he wore his gun belt tight at the waist, above the hip. Some other details about the man scratched for footholds in Maynard's mind.

He was supposed to remember something special about the kitchen at JJ's place, not this mouthy cowpoke.

Margins spoke up again. "Ain't you in a hurry to get who done in Dusty? Ain't you in a hurry to run a rope up on him, JJ? Was me I'd be out there chasin' him now." His hands rested on his hips, on his belt line, like it was his place got burned out. "I wouldn't be wastin' no time talkin' 'bout who I was after, that's for sure." Looking at the crowd around Maynard, he searched for sympathetic answers.

JJ said, "I'm not worried about catching the man those who did it. I don't want a whole bunch of riders, like in a crazy posse running all over my place."

"That's kind of funny talk, JJ. If your cows are gone, don't you want 'em back?"

"If they're gone to hell, we'll find them. I got Blue Feather, the Kiowa, down in the livery waiting on us. He can find any man who was on my spread if I let him be by himself. Hell, he can track Clutch here, right to the door when he fell in, looking for us. He sure didn't come here to dance, not from how I look at it."

Margins said, "How's that, JJ?"

"He came to tell us what he's forgot for the moment. We just sit patient with him and it'll all come back." JJ put his hand down to Maynard and brought him to his feet. "I'd get you another drink, Clutch, but I don't think I better. We'll get that later, if you've a mind. Try again about the kitchen. Mame did a bit of decorating before we left, sprucing things up."

Maynard tried to picture Mame at work in the kitchen. "What'd she do, JJ?" Then another picture came at him. "She a lefty, JJ?"

"No," JJ said. "Why?"

"If you and Mame aren't lefties, whoever was in your kitchen after you left for town had coffee and was a lefty. Before he torched the barn and whatever, he had coffee and he was a lefty. That's part of what I remember. The pot on the table was set down by a lefty. The cup was on the left side of the table. I don't know what made me notice, but it was like I felt keen all over noticing things. I knew I had to come tell you whenever I found you. I didn't want to be a dummy about things. I kept my eyes open. What did Mame do in the kitchen before you came to town? You said decorating."

JJ shook his head, saw round Mame at work. "Painted a couple of chairs. Mercy's getting married in a month and she's getting the place primed for company. "He looked around until he saw his daughter Mercy staring at him from the crowd. "Painted the chairs a dark red. Looked pretty good."

It was as if three men, JJ and Maynard and Margins, shared the same thought at the same instant. Maynard steady now on his feet, JJ's hands free of him, both noticed again the red smudges on Margins' pants, just as he started to back away and go for his gun, left-handed, across his mid-section, desperate, found out.

Maynard and JJ's guns were leveled at Margins' gut before his hand reached his gun. A big, rangy cowpoke, his night out for dancing interrupted by all the news, dropped his arms around Margins and locked Margins' arms in place. He was quick and powerful and looked very angry as he squeezed the breath out of the left-handed killer, the left-handed bushwhacker.

38

JJ put his arm on Maynard's shoulder. "Cows won't be hard to find. Blue Feather can do that in a shake. But we got a barn to build, a house to fix, and a wedding to get ready for. You're top man on the guest list, Clutch. What do you say to that."

"I thought I come here to do some slow dancing."

A snappy looking girl in a red dress stepped out of the crowd and took his hand. The fiddles started just as Dusty Twitchell's killer was dragged to the door by the sheriff and a deputy.

"Mommy," 4-year old Billy Baird yelled at midnight for the third night in a row. "I heard the horn again." An August night hung its heaviness over the ranch house, between mountains in Utah.

Billy's father Hal rolled over in bed and said, "Hannah, will you get him squared away. I did it last night, but I have corral work all day tomorrow. Would you please?" He patted her on the backside and rolled back where he had been sound asleep, and was soon gone that way again.

Hannah Baird had a blanket wrapped around her as she went to the little room where Billy was whimpering again about hearing horns in the night. It was the third night of hearing the horns and the boy was still restless, she thought.

On the way to him, pausing in the darkness, she heard nothing. Here, at the foot of the Wasatch Range, night was a silence broken only by an owl's call, a wolf's howl, the cry of a mountain cat, a horse's neigh, and the smell of night hot with the weather. The sounds were usual and disturbed nobody beyond the length of their echoes. At the southern end of the range, they could see high peaks from the window in the back of the ranch house.

And Billy, in the last month, had heard an old Ute Indian talking about ghosts that haunted the high range. The Indian had sat at a campfire, talking with Billy's father who had invited him to share in a range meal.

"The spirits of the dead let us know they are still here. They say that Senawahv, creator of all things, allows them to stay near their descendants. It is a move of justice to the good ones. I hope someday my voice will be heard in the night."

Hannah mentioned the Indian's talk, to provide a reason for not worrying.

But Billy came right back at her. "Not voices, Mommy, but a horn. I heard a horn again. Like I did last night." She surmised he was counting in his pause. "Like the other night too."

He had never been so imaginative, she thought; sleeping well most every night until the last few nights. In fact, he was a good sleeper from his first days. In his first month he had slept clean through on a few nights, which she and Hal had accepted gratefully.

"Were you sleeping, Billy? Did it wake you up?"

40

"No, Mommy. I was waiting for the horn. I heard it again, and the wind was blowing, too, very loud."

"Did the wind keep you awake until midnight?" She wondered about his perception of time.

"I was waiting for the horn. And I heard it."

"Mommy will sit with you and we'll listen awhile and then go to sleep."

He was asleep in a couple of minutes, nestled against his mother.

The next night he cried earlier, and louder, saying he had heard the horn louder than ever.

She held him until he was asleep, and when she tried to cover him for the remainder of the night, she was brought upright on the side of the bed. From a distance she heard it, the sound of a bugle or trumpet cutting through the night air as sharp as a knife, but distant and, she thought, almost holy. Bill ought to hear this, she said as if he could hear her. "Oh, he wouldn't believe what he was hearing anyway."

The horn sounded once more, and Billy slept through it all, the angelic face of her son a comfort to her as she wondered about what she had heard. She had, indeed, heard a horn. Billy had heard a horn, on four or five nights. It was eerie.

Hal Baird finished his work on a new corral late in the afternoon and said he had to go to town for more supplies. Hannah and Billy would spend the late afternoon in the kitchen. There was no talk about horns.

Asa Quince, Bountyville's lone storekeeper, said to Hal Baird and a few other customers, "Did you hear about the army patrol? They got set upon by some renegades up on Graves Hill. Three men got wounded and one man is missing. Nobody's seen him. They figure they'll have to get reinforcements before they go looking for his body up there. Man must be dead by now if he was wounded too. That post out there is so small it seems like the army don't count them at all. I think they send anybody who's at the end of the trail out here to finish up, them and some plain old losers they'd like to see get lost themselves."

Baird said, "You sure the army said they had to wait for reinforcements before they'll go looking for the lost trooper?"

"Right here in front of me, that cavalry captain said it, the one

41

looks like he died last week. He don't want to go anywhere but home, wherever that could be this side of the grass." Pausing, thinking of something that came late to mind, he added, "Said something strange, he did. Said what bothered him most was the trooper was his bugler, and missed him at Reveille and Call to Colors and such, like he was homesick."

Hal Baird, ex-Army of the Potomac, patriot, bristled and said, "That sure ain't fair what he says. Ought to break their butts looking for a man that did his bit no matter how the upper echelon looks at him. I saw some heroes couldn't shine their boots, but stood up to be counted when it was time to be counted. You don't forget them, no matter what they can or can't do."

The storekeeper thought that over, nodded, and said, "If I was a sprout again, Hal, I'd be up there looking, damned if I wouldn't. Chance to do some good before I check out on all this." The spread of his arms could have said Bountyville, Utah, the USA, the world. His listeners had their pick.

Out in front of the general store within the hour, Baird had a few good pals gathered at the corner of the general store. "We know that country up there better than the army does. All of us have spent long hours chasing down lost cattle, big cats too much on the edge of our herds; we've even gone fishing under the falls for the big ones. We ought to give it a chance. Give him one chance, whoever he is. They might not get any reinforcements for a month. If the man is wounded, losing or has lost blood, he won't last much longer than today or tomorrow or one more day."

"We don't even know if the man's alive, Hal," one old pard said. "He could have crawled off and died in half a day. Those mountains are tough for anybody."

Hal looked around, nodded at a thought, and said, "I got something to tell you, but you keep it quiet. My kid Billy has been hearing horns at night, right near midnight, for the last three nights I'd guess. Wake him right out of his sleep, wakes up crying about the horn blowing him awake."

"You saying what I think you're saying, Hal, that the missing man, the bugler, is up there someplace blowing the horn, needing help, trying to let us know? Why at midnight? How?"

"I've been thinking about that, maybe he does too, the bugler. Who hears such a thing in the day if we are busy at what we do? Or

42

pays attention to it. Too much going on around us. Too much noise. Cows and kids bawling. Horses' hooves pounding. Wheels turning. Women gabbing. Whatever. At midnight sound carries better, probably goes farther. Maybe he's only got so much energy left."

"By gosh, Hal, you got me roped in all the way. If Melba was still here she'd be goin' with us. One of the things made her the woman she was. That's special. Damned right I'll go."

The others said they'd join in. They planned to leave from Hal's place just before sun up.

When Baird told Hannah and Billy they were going to look for the horn player, Billy said, "Maybe he can play to bring the birds back when they leave."He was looking at the bird feeder on a fencepost when he said it. It was his one chore.

Brister Paulie, Hal Baird's oldest army buddy, brought a surprise ... his nephew Phil who carried a bugle on his saddle horn. "Just in case we have to wake the trooper up," Paulie said, winking at the others. "He don't play too good but he makes the thing work."

"Some folks in town think we're plain daft, Hal" but they don't laugh none around me when I'm bein' my best to be hard. But I didn't tell none of them about the bugle part. That's just for us."

Three hours later they were on a high trail going cross Graves Hill. It was an old Indian trail that three of the four men on the rescue trip had traveled before. Paulie's nephew Phil had never been this far up in the mountains. "Sure is pretty up here," he said as they rested their horses at one point.

"We ain't here for pretty, boy," Paulie said. "Let's hope we're doin' some good for a creature maybe who's dead already, maybe not."

They had been an hour on this one stretch of trail worn into Graves Hill for centuries. There was no place to hide that they had seen, if the trooper was hiding from the renegades, wild animals, other visitors if there were such. All the time Hal Baird could see his ranch house down in the valley, thinking of Billy hearing horns, possibly being played from this place, this edge of the mountain, for Graves Hill was indeed a mountain reaching for the sky.

He could tell the men were disappointed that they had not found the trooper. Yet he was somehow sure that the man had to be under cover, protected from the animals that roamed freely in the mountains. He envisioned wolves, cougars, bears, wild peccary that

43

could gore a man to death.

Life, at the outset, was chancy up here, at best.

There had to be cover. If the trooper was dead, they'd never know. If he was alive, they had to give it every shot. On an impulse, he asked Paulie's nephew to blow on the bugle. "Send something out, see if we get answer. It's a big place up here and we could look for a hundred years."

The nephew, with some difficulty, made some noise with the bugle. The sound, not quite musical, bounced off the cliffs and rock peaks all around them, echoed like a streamer in a parade, then died out, faint as faint could be.

Nothing happened. There was no response, no bugle call of any sort from the mountain itself. The silence itself almost died out. An eagle screamed beyond them. A wolf answered the disturbance.

A horse snickered, and then another in answer.

Paulie looked seriously at Baird, shook his head and said, "Nothin' I can hear. Hope you got better ears than me." He was shaking his head and tossing his shoulders and moving his arms, all in desperate gestures.

An eagle, from overhead, broadcast its whereabouts.

All the men sat motionless on their horses, as if in prayer or contemplation.

In the absolute silence that followed then, at the end of a heartbeat, of a tonal island found in the ears, a whisper of a horn came to them as if from the face of the cliff opposite them on the trail. It was faint, a pale imitation of a real horn.

"It's coming from over there," said Paulie's nephew, standing in his stirrups, pointing, "but I don't see any caves there.

Baird swung his mount around and scanned the length of the trail on the near side. "Up there, or down there and it's bouncing off that other side. Spread out and look, but keep quiet. Tie your mounts off."

Even as he spoke, the distant, faint sounds came to him. The bugler was alive, but hidden, somewhere on the trail. In a cave, under an overhang, hanging on for dear life."

Paulie's nephew Phil, caught up in the drama, blew out a couple of notes, his hands shaking, his eyes wide open as he blew into the bugle again.

There was his echo, and then a faint answer.

Hal Baird, moving as quickly as he could, scoured places on the trail, and then saw the fissure behind a shelf of rock that had slipped off the face of the cliff.

He stuck his head into the darkness. "Are you in here, trooper?" He held his breath.

"Corporal Brogan, sir, and glad you came by. I've been wounded, hurting, hungry, but feel as good right now as I've ever felt. You wouldn't have a spare drink on you, would you?"

"A one-time sergeant, here, Corporal, with nothing except warm water in a canteen, but I can promise all you want once we get downhill to my place. What say to that?"

"I'm sure happy I brought my bugle. Is that what brought you up here? We really got scattered by some renegades, and they got me in the leg. I had three days of trail chow with me, and found a leak in the mountain right in here. Got a cup a day out of it. Got me to my bugle at night, thinking it would be heard best then. Scared some animals plain outright other times."

"My boy Billy, he's only four, will be happy to meet you, Corporal. He's the reason we're up here. The horn scared him silly some nights. When you're having that drink I promised, you can thank him."

"I'll play for him, Sarge, but can I do it at high noon?"

"High noon is just about perfect, Corporal," Baird said. He wished he had a watch.

His name was Roscoe Drummond, a rugged, quick-spirited veteran of the Great War that lay in shambles at his feet as he prepared to take off his uniform. The sounds of war had almost disappeared from the air about him, though he had been wounded twice on the very last day of the war. Blood now crusted on his uniform as he sprawled in the hay of a barn, ready to don some clothes he had already stripped from a clothesline when the second stray round hit him. The shot had been meant for the man who was now stretched out in the barnyard. The dead man's pleas had not been heeded by his killers, their thinking the war would go on forever, as if war was their due, war was their passion.

All of it was a sign, he believed, a sign that would send him on a mission for the remainder of his life.

In the barn where he had hidden from the search party that killed the barn owner, his mind fixed the mission in his life even as he heard screaming from the farmhouse. Drummond did not change into the farmer's clothes, but hustled his best to get to the house as the screams of women continued.

The two soldiers in the house, with the utmost terror in their hearts, had frightened a mother and daughter out of their wits, and had tied them up in one room. Bound on committing their next crime, in the same uniform that Drummond wore, which infuriated him, he shot both men on the spot, freed the women, and buried the husband and the two soldiers. He told the women not to mention the soldiers to anyone. In some of the farmer's clothes he departed, on a horse given to him by the farmer's widow, the ravages of the war behind him, the wide open west waiting on the far horizon.

A month later, and a month past a wagon train send-off station in Missouri, Drummond cleared the top of a hill, hurrying to investigate rapid gunfire ahead of him on the trail. A lone Conestoga wagon was circled by five men firing at will into the body of the wagon. With dead aim, his rifle over the remnants of a blow-down on top of the hill, he dropped two riders from the saddle and wounded a horse that limped away with the rider jumping off to hide behind a rock. When the roadside brigands started returning his fire, a fusillade of shots came from the wagon and two of the robbers fled on horseback. The third man raised his hands in surrender and

46

stepped out from behind the rock. He was shot dead on the spot with one round from the wagon.

A woman, of perhaps thirty years of age, in a calico dress, stepped down from the wagon, the rifle still in her hands, gunpowder fumes seeping from the barrel. A boy of ten years stepped down with her, and then a smaller girl. It was evident the three of them were stunned. The children were clutching at the woman's person.

The woman shouted uphill at Drummond, "He killed my husband, the children's father. I saw him do it, that man there." She pointed at the man she had just killed, sprawled on the ground, final movements at turmoil in his body.

Drummond, riding down, said, "What are you doing out here. Where's the wagon train."

"We had to stop to fix a wheel. My husband said something was done to the wheel and the others left. Said we could catch up to them."

"What kind of wagon master would do that?" Drummond said.

"My husband said he had no right to do it. Nobody else said a word, like they knew something was coming along the way. It was as if they felt the whole trip was going to be dismal, a failure. I thought such folk would have better spirit."

Drummond marveled at her stand. "You bound on continuing your trip?"

"Yes, we are. We have relatives waiting on us in Texas. My brother went on a head a few months ago. He just got out of the Army of the Republic. He was a major in the war. His name was Diction."

"Larry Diction?" said a surprised Drummond stepping down from the saddle. "I knew a Larry Diction from Marblehead, outside of Boston, from a sailing family. That can't be him, can it, a sailor heading west?"

"That's him. I think the President sent him on some special mission. He would not say a word about it. How do you know him?"

"He was in my regiment in the army. He was a good soldier. If the president picked him, he was a good judge of character. I met him twice, both times near Shiloh." Carrying explanations further, he said, "My name is Roscoe Drummond, at your service, Ma'am."

"Where are you bound, Mr. Drummond? My name is Mrs. Peter Preble, once Laura Diction, of Marblehead."

47

"Well, my first mission is to get you caught up with the wagon train," and then he said, which brought a wide smile to her face, "to ask that wagon master why he left you folks out her on the trail. So, let's get that wheel fixed and do some catching up. Though I'm afraid we'll have to take care of the burying right here."

The woman was aghast, when she asked, "In the same ground?"

"There's only this ground, Ma'am. It'll have to do."

With the wheel fixed, the burying all done for the dead, words said over each grave at Drummond's insistence, the wagon caught up with the wagon train the next evening. Drummond lit into the wagon master, letting all his anger come into play.

The wagon master was not at all apologetic. "If you dally for one wagon, you dally for all. It's not fair to the others."

"You didn't think of leaving one man or two with them, with a woman and two children and only her husband to watch over them?"

"I didn't even consider it. I've lead four trains over this same ground and that's how I've done it. If you want to ride with us, you'll have to do what I say. I am the wagon master. I go by the name of Chesapeake Jaynes, from Baltimore originally."

"Well, Chesapeake," Drummond said, "I had to kill two men back there who I'm sure messed up the wagon so it'd break down after it left the station, and Mrs. Preble had to shoot the man who killed her husband. That's a pretty poor start for a family, and for this train. I'll pass on the job opportunity and move on ahead by myself. But I believe that's not the end of those men. Two of them rode off after three of them were killed. I'm betting they'll come after you again, but with more bodies. There's something here that they want, I'm thinking. Five men against one man are pretty good odds, like someone was looking for a solid edge on success."

"What could that be?"

"I have no idea," Drummond said, "but I think you'll find out. It might well be the Preble wagon was a special target from the start." He proceeded to tell the Jaynes about Mrs. Preble's brother. "He's now out in Texas on a mission of sorts, from what she says. From the President, maybe. It's intriguing from the first thought, politics being what it is, the war being over, all the west out there beyond us like a piece of land come up when the tide went out and no flag on it."

He looked at Jaynes and added, "Of course you know this is between me and you and no other soul in creation, or I'll come down on you worse than you've ever felt. That's a scared promise, from me to you. Take it serious, Chesapeake."

He climbed into the saddle, nodded at the wagon master, and repeated his words, "I'll be out front on my own. Watch the ground as you go. Never can tell what's out there. Do you have a good scout ahead?"

"Good as they get. He can smell injuns and hyenas if they're in the way. Let him know who you are, you bounden to go on alone. He calls himself Herbie Sawyer and he's about big enough to ride a pony in the first place, but he's got hawk's eyes and rabbit ears and can shoot the cover of a can of peaches at a hundred yards." He smiled for the first time and said, "More or less."

"I'll say hello to Herbie for you, Chesapeake," Drummond promised as he headed his horse down-range towards a wide expanse of grass, and a river with fast running water at the end of the grass and a range of mountains on the northern edge of the prairie.

Drummond reflected on a lot of things he had seen in the late part of the day; the sun sat on the peaks of the mountain as if they were on fire, and a breeze carried the smell of water to every head of stock in the wagon train, causing a bit of unrest. That stock included horses, mules, a few oxen, and a few dairy cows almost as precious as the horses. In addition, there were some chicks newly hatched, more eggs on hand, a few bunnies in cages, and a dozen roosters that made dawn as clear as possible. Drummond admired the extent of the promise the wagon people carried with them, to enrich the life at the end of the journey.

As he rode along ahead of the wagon train, alert to all movement, he kept thinking about Preble's mission, what it meant, and where life was taking him … his wounds all healed, newer clothes fitting properly, and a new saddle most likely to be under him for as long as he rode a horse.

After an hour's ride ahead, in a small copse of cottonwoods off to the side of the trail, he saw a slight movement, and slipped into a shallow swale, and approached the copse from the rear. Even before he was there, he caught sight of the wagon train scout sitting his saddle, eyes on the trail where he had been. The scout swung easily in his saddle and greeted Drummond. "I saw you slip down in

49

that wadi and knew you were coming in behind me, Mister. You have good intentions or not? His rifle was trained on Drummond.

"Chesapeake Jaynes asked me to say hello, Herbie. Name's Roscoe Drummond. Said not to miss you 'cause you wouldn't miss me. You see anything of a couple or more hombres obviously out for no good except their own? I'm sure they'll be along this trail somewhere with only their interests at heart."

"That's why I'm sitting in here, Roscoe, 'cause I seen six riders skirting us back there, keeping off a good measure from the wagons but not seeing me, from where I've been sitting. Seen them a couple or more times and them keeping out of sight like they was trying to find a good spot to say hello in their own way. One of them's always practicing his fast draw, which ain't too good yet, like he's anxious to meet Mr. Death."

"Well, Herbie, for putting information aside, what's he look like?"

"That's easy, Roscoe. Can pick him out from here if I saw them now. Wears a funny hat you don't see this way. Like a opera hat or a hat Abe would have wore. Black and tall, like the neck on a wood stove."

Drummond told Sawyer his suspicions about the men and the president sending Larry Diction on a special assignment out to the far west. "I think it's all connected somehow. There's something in the Preble wagon or in one of the wagons of the train that they want, or what they were sent for. I don't believe for one minute they want to get rich or even comfortable with what they could take from the train. Let's wait until it gets a little darker and walk in on them softly before they walk in on the wagon or charge like Indians not afraid of the dark."

"That's a good idea, Roscoe. You kinda think like I do. Let's get some rest. We'll toss fingers for first watch." Herbie won the first watch and Roscoe Drummond was asleep in minutes, his horse watered and rubbed down, his saddle sitting on the ground, sweet pillow of dreams.

Two hours later, Sawyer woke Drummond easily, a finger touching him after he spoke his name. "Roscoe, there's two of them coming in on us from opposite sides. I went right out in front when you went to sleep, through high grass and sat like a rabbit waiting. They're coming straight in from each side, there and there, "and he pointed out the two directions. "You take him and I'll take him," he said, "and if we do it without any noise, I'd real appreciate it." Then he added, "Tall Hat's not with them."

Drummond nodded and smiled and slipped off into the grass, their two horses sitting still as trained pups.

Sawyer said he clubbed his man from behind, when he and his prisoner came into camp, and Drummond had his man gagged with a kerchief and his hands bound with a twist of wire he carried in a pocket. He'd fished with the wire, snared a few rabbits, tied up three different prisoners of war, once even using it as a tourniquet. Now he had a private prisoner trussed tight and sure, and a bit of pain with a single twist of the wire.

"Here's what we do, Herbie," Drummond said. "Don't let them look into each other's face as we question them. Keep the gag on your man while I question my prisoner, for one of them has to tell us what's going on."

It did not take many questions or many twists of the wire before the man answered questions about their mission.

"Some big landowner in Texas, I don't know his name, none of us do, sent us for a document the president is sending about Texas. We're looking for the man who is carrying it, name of Diction. That's all I know except we were promised a thousand a piece to get it. There's ten of us all told. Now I suppose I don't get a dime of it."

"You get nothing, man. Diction's been in Texas for more than a month and he's using a different name. Probably walked right by you and your pals on the way. So you and your gang best head back that way. We'll let you go now, without your weapons. You can walk out. We'll keep your horses for a while and leave them tied up and easy enough to find tomorrow. Don't come looking for us, for we've had five men of our own spotting you all the time. Some of us are sitting almost on top of your pals now. Best tell them to cut and run."

The two men, less weapons, horses, gags, and the trusty piece of wire, walked away from the copse of trees, heading across the prairie.

Sawyer, smiling like a bandit himself who had just tricked somebody out of their wealth, said, "Roscoe, you got a ton of tricks. I don't think those folks will try us on again, us and our own gang." He laughed heartily as they headed away from the copse, the prairie dark, a westerly wind soft as a woman's breath on their cheeks, and the stars glittering in spatial comfort.

Drummond played a vital role in two more escapades involving the safety of the wagon train crossing half of Texas, in league with Chesapeake Jaynes and Herbie Sawyer.

Never was he very far from Laura Preble and her two children during that time. He would make a habit of it once she set up her living arrangements, he promised himself, and would eventually meet her brother again and find out what the real plans were for Texas.

The rider sat awkwardly in the saddle as he came onto the Benedict Road, his horse moving as though he was hobbled. Clara Wilson, at the reins of the ranch wagon, her father flat in the back of the wagon after a visit to Doc Traverse in town, eased her own horse to a halt. The rider, in a gray sombrero, black vest and faded gray shirt, did not notice her approach. Clara had a rifle at hand, but did not reach for it. As ever she was ready for surprises, recalling at that instant her grandmother saying happiness and sadness come in the strangest shapes and at the strangest times. She wondered if this was one of those times.

In the rear of the wagon her father moaned a soft protest about the bumpy road. Out in front of her, in the middle of the road, the stranger fell off his horse and lay still in the dust.

Clara, with rifle in hand, as if the act was a ruse, approached on foot the fallen man whose eyes remained closed but whose breathing was apparent. Such a good looking young man, she thought, as she checked his pulse, moved his head so she could get a better look at his face. Besides being handsome, she knew he was hurting as the moan escaped from his lips, a shiver shook his body. A strange silver medallion was clipped to his shirt, appearing to read $FR/1^{st}RR$ on a star shape. Clara had never seen anything like it and had no idea of what it was or what it represented. In her 18 years she had never been beyond the ranch and the little town of Benedict, at the foot of the Tetons.

It was too far to go back to town. She'd have to take him to the ranch. With some difficulty she managed to get him onto the wagon beside her father, who stared at her and the new passenger and said, "You be careful, Clara. We never saw this man before. Better give me the rifle. I can hold it close on him."

"He's really hurting, Pa," she said, and climbed back behind the reins, set her feet, and set the horse off on a gallop to home. "We'll get him home and send somebody for Doc Traverse."

Only two hours earlier, Boyd Hardy Forsyth, cowboy in search of work, had been riding free and easy at the edge of a slight forested rise at the foot of the mountain. The sun was shining brightly, he could hear birds singing above him in the tree line, and his mount was freshly watered, brushed down and fed. A sense of comfort touched him, and then a bullet tore into his side from an unknown source. Amazement hit him also; he had seen no riders for half a day, heard no gunfire, and expected none. His horse bolted and Forsyth had to hold tight to stay in the saddle, knowing he had little control over the animal. In seconds he was bent over the pommel, barely keeping himself on the horse that took him through a copse of trees, sundry brush, and through a canyon full of echoes of his horse's shoes.

No other shots followed the first one, but he knew he was far from safe because of the blood he was losing. He grabbed the pommel tighter, felt light-headed, and feared falling from the saddle.

He woke in a bed in the ranch house of Carl Wilson, recuperating rancher who had been gored by a wild steer, and was being ministered to by a young girl and an elderly man who said he was a doctor. For the second or third time that day, all surroundings faded away and this time he lapsed into a deep sleep, hearing no more of the conversation that swirled around him.

The doctor said, "He rode right out of the trees and collapsed on the road, Clara? No warning? No yelling? Nobody chasing him? Rather strange, don't you think?" He stood beside the bed and shook his head.

"Doc," Carl Wilson said, "you ask more questions without waiting for an answer than my dear departed Alma ever threw at me. What Clara said is just the way it happened. It was a strange encounter, needless to say, and Clara acted as any Good Samaritan would. She's an angel like her mother was. And you know that as well as I do."

"You know damned well, Carl, that I loved her as long as you did. There's no mystery about that. She was a very special lady and Clara is following in her footsteps, plain and simple. But this is still a mystery. For all we know he might be an outlaw on the run and some posse gunner might have taken a shot at him. It doesn't look like an accident to me. It just doesn't happen like this, out in nowhere. Nor does it end up here in the bed of an old friend of mine. There is more coming to this, mark my words." The doctor paused and added, "And what in tarnation is this thing he's wearing on his shirt?"

"There you go, Doc, with more questions. We don't have any idea. Clara asked me too, right off, and I have never seen anything like it. And, I might add, I have no idea at all about it."

54

The doctor said, "It has to be some kind of affiliation, perhaps military, but nothing like anything around here, at Fort Albion or even at the command post back on the river."

Clara interjected, "I don't think he's an outlaw. I don't think any posse member shot him and then just didn't follow up. Besides, he's too handsome to be wrong." She made another judgment and added, "At anything."

Her father and the doctor raised their eyebrows, nodded and squeezed their lips in agreement … with each other.

Forsyth woke early in the morning, a persistent ache doing the wakening, dryness in his throat. Clara stood in the doorway as he stirred awake, a coffee pot in her hands. He thought she was the prettiest picture he had seen in a long time.

"Well, whatever your name is, I have hot coffee for you, and interest mounting all the time about who you are. Somebody asked if you might be an outlaw shot by a posse. I said I didn't believe you were. My name is Clara Wilson and you are in my father's house at the end of the Benedict Road. We found you on the road. You fell off your horse. We have him in the corral. He's okay."

Forsyth shook his head and mustered a smile. "Thank you, Clara Wilson, for being so good to me. I am not an outlaw and don't know who shot at me. My name is Boyd Forsyth and I was just looking for work in one of the ranches down this way from Benedict. One gent told me there was work out this way. I met him when I was getting a shave."

Clara smiled at that revelation, seeing how clean shaven he was, and good looking.

Forsyth, stroking his chin, said, "That must have been yesterday, but I'm not really sure. How long have I been here?" Around the room he looked, seeing the décor and the set-up of the room. There was no denying whose room it was, for it spoke so clearly of this girl had brought him to her home, who now stood so pretty in the doorway waiting to wait on him. He blushed a little thinking he was in Clara Wilson's bed.

"You've only been here overnight," she said, and resolved any doubts by adding, "I slept on the couch for the night. Chances are my parents will rush you out of here today and settle you in the bunkhouse. If you want work we have a job here."

Her mother called as she entered the room. "How's our guest

doing, Clara? He feeling better?"

"Oh, yes, Ma'am," Forsyth said and noticed the receptive smile on the face of each woman. "Nice and comfortable, and my wound feels much better. Did the doctor remove the bullet?"

"Yes, he did," said Mrs. Wilson. "Doc Traverse is his name and he said it was a little difficult, but he made do. He generally does. He was also wondering about that attachment you wear on your shirt, as does everybody else. Do you mind if I ask what it is?" She had placed her hands on her hips, like the lady of the house would only expect a true answer.

"Not a bit, Ma'am. I wear it honor of my grandfather's army outfit, Forsyth's Rifles which he modeled after the First Regiment of Rifles, United States Army. That's what the FR/1stRR stands for. It's a silver replica. The unit, in 1812 and '13, was stationed in northern New York under his command, Captain Benjamin Forsyth. They sought to provide protection against British troops in the surrounding areas and to keep a lookout for British military movements.

That evening, as supper was just over, Clara's father, Carl Wilson, said, "Son, we have word about a bank robbery back down the road you came from. The description of the man sure does not fit you, but me and Doc Traverse have a theory about some of what's gone on here."

Forsyth said, "And you think I'm involved in it?" He looked at Clara with a worried look. "I swear I've done no wrong, sir."

"Oh," Clara said, "we believe you, Boyd. It's just something else they've been thinking about, or cooking up just to ask each other a bunch of questions. Been doing it most of their lives. Real inquisitive, the pair of them."

"It involves me getting shot?"

"It does, son," Wilson said, "but we have settled on a very curious explanation."

"I'd like to hear that, sir, especially the part of me not being directly involved."

"Oh, I didn't say not directly involved, you were that, but not in the holdup of the bank, or the death of a teller and a customer, but you did get shot, son."

"I don't understand any of it now, sir," Forsyth slid in, shaking his head, shrugging his shoulders.

Clara jumped in before he father could answer. "At first we

56

thought you had been shot by a posse and managed to escape them, and your wound wore you down so you fell in the road right off the saddle. They have come up with something else all together." She smiled, as if all his problems were over, just as his hands touched the softness of the material so that he could remember it ever after.

"Yes, Boyd," Wilson said. "When we realized you didn't fit the description of the robber, and didn't get shot at by a posse, we thought maybe the robber thought you were part of a posse and shot you."

"Why would you think that, or why him think that?" Forsyth shook his head again.

"Simply because that piece you were wearing on your shirt, being real silver as you say, catches the sun just like a deputy or a sheriff's badge would, or a marshal's badge. The robber and killer must have known that someone would be on his trail sooner or later, with all the mess he was running from. He saw the shine of it and figured it was a badge." He paused and then asked, "Do you remember exactly where you were when the bullet hit you? He might have a hideout somewhere near there."

Forsyth thought a while, about the lay of the land, where he had last watered his horse, where the tree line was the thickest in the day's ride. A small crop of rock overhang came into his mind. A large bird, maybe a vulture had been circling high overhead. The bones of a dead animal were strewn on the ground.

"Yes, I could find that place again if you took me right back to where you found me, give me a starting point."

"Yes," Clara said, clapping her hands. "We'll get you right back in the same wagon and go back there. Such a short ride it was. It was quicker and safer for you to get you home here, like I said before."

"I'd rather ride my horse, Clara, if you don't mind."

"Well, not today anyway, son," Carl Wilson said. "We'll give you another night's rest if Clara doesn't mind giving up her bed for one more night."

"Not at all, Pa," Clara said, and her father knew she had strengthened her rights of possession, the smile on her face, the light in the young man's eyes. His own history came rushing through him.

Just as dawn broke the next day, the sun coming over the eastern hills, the unofficial posse from the Wilson Ranch moved slowly into the area as Forsyth pointed out a few points of interest that he had remembered. It had been an easy ride for him, with only a slight discomfort from his healing wound.

The seven riders, almost at the same instance, held their horses in place as the aroma of morning coffee and burnt biscuits filled the air. The swirl of smoke, above them in the maize of rocks, catastrophic falls and old blow downs, spiraled upward in a thin stream.

Not a shot was fired as five men crept right up on the robber-killer as he munched on his breakfast, five weapons drawn and pointed, and a click from one weapon as he wiped his mouth with his sleeve, and stared at the bores of the pointed weapons.

You know the story about Boyd Hardy Forsyth from then on, how he worked as a drover for Carl Wilson, married his daughter Clara, raised a family, and became the marshal of the territory, all after getting the $500 reward for a desperate bank robber and killer. On his chest he wore the marshal's badge and continued to wear the old silver testament to his grandfather's service to the country, the one that looked like another badge.

The old man, beggar of drinks, spittoon cleaner, dung shoveler, was shot and killed behind the livery. Taylor Maxon rushed from his card game. He was kneeling over the town drunk when the others came from the card game. "He's dead," Maxon said, "and he said he felt a whole lot of curses coming right up from his belly and then he said Shearwell did it. In his last breath he said Shearwell did it. Called him a liar and then shot him." He looked up from where he still knelt over the dead man. "I heard a galloper heading out of town. Round up a posse!"

That little burp of light in the morning's pre-dawn sky could always twinkle Luke Shearwell awake from the deepest sleep, out on the prairie, at a branding campsite, on a line fence by himself. All that after a full day in the saddle and a late plate of beans and steak on the run. He and the star had a history of sorts. And on this day of flight it would rouse him once again from sleep on the small ledge where he was hidden from the posse.

It didn't matter that Luke Shearwell had not done anything wrong except run from the posse's wild bunch headed, of course, by Taylor Maxon, who'd been in love with Laura Mordant long before Luke had come along. Maxon had practically demanded the deputy's badge from the sheriff of the growing town of Canyon. "You need all the help you can get, sheriff, 'cause there's something going on around us. I can feel it and I know you can. Too much trouble when it should be quiet. Little guys getting squeezed by big guys. Rustlers. Mysterious ranch house fires in the night. You need another good gun at your side." He nodded his head in that cocky way he had as he added, "and a decision-maker wearing the badge. You'd get that in me and everybody's for it. I fit in this town. I always have." And then he capped his stance off with what could be called a marquee statement of the times in The Panhandle: "There are too many 'big Interest' outfits looking at all the assets in The Panhandle, including all of Palo Duro Canyon."

Maxon, for all his bluster, sat well on a horse, could shoot the spokes off a wheel at 60 feet, no mean feat for anybody in the saddle, and had captured one bushwhacker in the middle of his act. Some of the townsfolk said, with enough time under his belt, Maxon would

59

have the stuff to become the governor of the state… his name floating always in good tidings. He never personally affirmed that such aims were in his saddlebags, and only smiled at the rumors.

What Taylor Maxon really wanted, besides Laura Mordant, and the huge spread out there in the Palo Duro Canyon that Colley Mordant was building, was getting newcomer Luke Shearwell out of the way. Too many times in the too few days he'd been in town had Laura's eyes drifted from conversation with Maxon to find the newcomer Shearwell never far away. That was enough to get under Maxon's skin early on.

And Mordant's ranch, being almost half the size of the whole Palo Duro Canyon, was a sign of the times. Big spreads had taken bites out of every little spread in the territory. Some of the takings did indeed smell from afar with more than wood smoke. As it happens, rumor and distrust went hand in hand.

Shearwell was looked upon by many citizens as just another saddle tramp who swung his leg off the saddle for a quick drink at the first saloon he came to and had got himself stuck in the little town of Canyon.

Canyon, new and growing, having a sheriff and no deputies, was also in The Panhandle, not far from the Palo Duro Canyon. Its stretch marks were not noticed by its own citizens, some of whom had slept right through its birth.

With comfort easing out of his body as night moved across the flat plains and the slight hills where he bivouacked, Shearwell shifted his head again on the edge of his saddle and crossed his ankles. His blanket felt warm and the position change offered temporary suspension of aches that had not really gone away after his hectic ride. At the site his boots were as close to him as his rifle, and just as necessary. The posse, he supposed, was still camped out there, resting for the night, getting ready for morning's resumption of the hunt, Maxon cracking the whip over their heads. If he could drive Shearwell into a lopsided gunfight, things would be a lot easier when it came to Laura. At the least, he could bring Shearwell into the jail, and there was no telling what could happen from then on, with him holding the keys.

Yet Luke Shearwell had been a step ahead of Maxon. And he had a good idea of what was happening, not only in the whole of the Panhandle, but what Maxon was up to from the beginning.

60

Luke Shearwell, in the darkness, studied the stars. As usual, they came with connections of all kinds... stories, directions, an opponent's plans at the end of deep thought, lighting the way home from a dark or perilous journey. He trusted them as he trusted his horse; those above him, imperial in a way, that under him, provincial in a way. He calculated his position. He planned his moves.

On the edge of the little shelf of rock he had selected to rest upon, his horse snickered and kicked at the hard surface, but it was the view that satisfied Luke's look out for horse traffic. During long stretches earlier in the night he had looked for flames flickering from a camp fire, and saw nothing. Nor had he smelled any coffee aroma riding the cool air of a September night. But intuition of a restless order kept working on him, and the sly and solitary messages that seemed to slip into his consciousness from that intuition kept saying, "Before the morning star." Like a toothache while in the saddle, or the sore rump at the other end of his small world, the words kept coming back to him. They were not new, those words. Hardly new.

For much of his life he had heard them handed to him as if on a family platter.

"Before the morning star."

He wanted to close his eyes for a while more, find a decent rest for mere minutes. It would do him the greatest good later on. But he kept hearing the same words. It made him move without closing his eyes. He rolled his blanket, saddled Plunger, slipped off the rim before daylight could circle his frame, strike his silhouette. The breeze was like a drink of water, cool, from deep in a well of sorts. He swore he could taste it in his throat.

Overhead he looked again, saw the star where it belonged since forever, and said, "Before the morning star." A pause was followed by, "Yes, sir, I'm moving before the morning star moves." He was speaking to an old man in his past, his grandfather. A vague image came to mind. But he heard the voice again, fresh, urgent: "Before the morning star."

There was so much more that Shearwell knew. When he looked into Plunger's eyes, he was looking at hundreds of years into the past when Plungers' forebears had come up out of Mexico with the Spanish explorer Coronado. The Indians, from down where Coronado had come, called the star the "Dawn Star." And the Comanche and Kiowa and other Plains Indians, who got the "gift of

61

horses" from Coronado, knew all along that many stories had come along with Coronado's horses. They knew some of the stories that were being carried in horses' eyes, as well as some of the magic and some of the kinship between horse and rider. It was enough confirmation for Shearwell that the star could be seen in Plunger's eyes.

He slipped off the rim, thought of a providential route out of his troubles, and again brought all of Canyon to mind. Laura Mordant was right in the middle of it.

What had bothered the town fathers, so to speak, was Shearwell's knowledge of the territory, the whole Panhandle and what made it tick, and it frightened them for a drifter to be so well-informed. The banker and a couple of big spread owners were more than upset, calling him a malingering upstart and rumor monger. Sodholme the banker thought him to be highly suspicious. A few of Shearwell's words hung on him and caused him deep unrest: "That ranch out there in the Palo Duro Canyon that Mordant's building is big as hell and is a sign of the times."

Some of his other observations, spoken out loud in Canyon saloons, made certain high-deal customers uneasy, like the night he carried on in the Dead Wagon Saloon:

"Way, way back, the Spaniard Coronado brought horses with him on his long walks and those ponies ended up a couple a hundred years later bred to Plains beauties by the Comanche and the Apache and the Kiowa. When the Indians were sent to reservations, the sheep and cattle war started and this little spot called Canyon grew and big ranches came along."

He could carry on for hours:

"When the Indians got to the reservations and the buffalo were practically wiped off the Plains, we saw sheep come into the region from south of us, just the way that Coronado came. Everything and everybody came this way. The railroad is coming too. Why? What's here beside tough weather and flat land and a couple of rivers running loose? I saw it all east a ways and it's headed here in a dozen or so years, that'll get some gents scratching for open land. That big ranch out there is bringing new times with it. Mark my words. Cattle life, as we know it, is going to change. Good old politics is going to crowd us, for damn sure. And any little guy that gets in the way."

Shearwell was too much to take, having come down right off a

62

dirty, old saddle after a long dirty ride. He was marked as if a branding iron had been heated just for him.

Maxon's deep-seated interests took over and the town, in its own sleepy way, kept its eyes closed. That's much of the reason why the posse was so fast in getting after Luke Shearwell, when they should have waited until morning to study trail sign.

When Luke Shearwell finished off reading the stars, especially the morning star, and decided what course of actions he would take, there was one location that offered the best options. He rode fast for Lookout Mound and tethered Plunger in a thick copse of cottonwoods. He put down his bed with a small log as a head rest, lit a small fire and let it smoke a bit, and sought a place to watch the trail he had left.

It was Maxon, ahead of the posse of course, who came up on the trail, looped his horse's reins about a rock, and walked to within rifle shot of the campsite. The sleeping form was easily seen alongside the fire. From his position, Maxon leveled his rifle at the form, looked back over his shoulder, saw a few shadows of the posse coming along the trail. When he hit the target dead center with two quick shots, he screamed at the lead men in the posse. "I got him. He went for his rifle and I got him. I got the killer as he was going for his rifle right beside him." He was exultant.

They rode in on the campfire, still smoldering. Two riders dropped down off their mounts and approached the form on the ground, their side arms in hand.

One of them yelled out, "Hey, Taylor, there's no one here. Just a blanket and a saddle bag rolled up. There's no rifle here. Thought you said he was goin' for his gun. There's only a stick here. You gotta be seein' things. You shoot a couple of holes in a blanket and give the man no chance? You want Shearwell that bad, you go get him yourself. I'm goin' back to town. I don't want none of this."

The two men mounted their horses, rode back to the balance of the posse coming up on them, and the whole posse, after a few minutes of talk, headed back to town.

Maxon was alone... until Luke Shearwell stepped out of the darkness, his rifle leveled at the new deputy.

"When you get all your explaining done, Maxon, I got a few surprises for you. The whole state of Texas has a surprise for you. I come right from the governor, and you can explain to him about

63

some of the stuff that's going on out here. He'll be glad to hear it. And I guess someone in town will be able to make a decision right soon."

He looked off as the morning star vanished with grace into blue skies coming alive.

John Joseph "Jack" Mabry, wrangler for the Cross-Bed Ranch in the Texas Panhandle, was as outspoken as any wrangler could be, demanding that his horses be given their honest due and good care "lest that cowpoke not doin' so be fixed one way or another. I ain't raisin' and runnin' chickens for the drive, but horses good as men and smarter that some I've known."

Cowboys, we know, can say a hundred ways they're in love, and here are a few of them:

He weren't born, mister, he was made for me. Just for me. My horse.

Now tell me that ain't some critter he's sittin' like he's on top of the world. That's a horse.

You think she's got a chest. See what my horse brings with her.

See how he runs, the way his muscles move him along, like the good Lord took special attention.

I'd put everythin' I own in the kitty, 'ceptin' my horse.

I'm sorry, Ma'am, but there's only one love in my life right now, and it's my horse.

Mabry was in the Hard Drive Saloon in Chapstown, the latest cattle drive for the Cross-Bed done and wrapped up, and was "dryin' out a bit o' the dust." The saloon was packed with people, many of the drovers from the Cross-Bed in the crowd.

One ornery cowpoke from another ranch, in a loud voice as if saying at first, "I'm a big teaser," actually said to Mabry, "Hey, Jack, I hear you'd rather kiss that horse of yours out front than a lady up the stairs." He nodded at the set of stairs against the far wall and dumped off one of those "I've-done-him-good-for-now" grins. His name was Jake Parlee.

Mabry finished off his beer and said, "I'd kiss him a hundred times 'fore I'd kiss that ugly face of yours, Parlee, and you can bet on that." And in the same moment warded off the punch Parlee threw back at him, slammed him on the jaw with one punch, and watched as he dropped to the floor. "A good horseman don't talk like that in mixed company, and him being the mixed company."

Addressing the whole saloon, knowing he had everybody's attention, Mabry said, "Just take a look at us, each one of us, and we ain't the same without our horse, without those reins in our hands, that powerful body under us. I think our friend Parlee here knows that like we all do, but he's got to find a way to make it known and not just tell his horse when he's alone out on the trail or ridin' guard or doing fence ridin'. It's the only way we can really share our horse, less'n a pal's mount goes down and he has to put it out of misery."

Mabry, the barkeep, and the crowd of cowpokes sat around for ten full minutes before the cowpoke Parlee regained his senses, stood up groggily and gingerly, picked up his hat and walked out of the saloon. There was no mean look over his shoulder, no "I'll get you for this" and no "We'll meet down the trail sometime."

It was cut and dried over, between horsemen, of one sort of another.

Or it ought to have been.

Two days later, in the evening shadows out on the trail between the Cross-Bed and Chapstown, some bushwhacker from the deepest shadows took a shot at Mabry, narrowly missing him. Mabry, firing back a spread of shots, not having seen a thing but figuring where the shot came from, ducked low in the saddle and lit out for town and the sheriff.

"I ain't sayin' Parlee did it, Sheriff, but he's as close to wanting me dead now as any I knowed this whole time. He should know better'n talk down a man's horse. It ain't a fittin' thing to do, him ridin' a horse all day like I do most days, bein' a cowpoke, herdin', drivin', runnin' with them great legs under your butt."

"You figure you got an idea where that shot come from, Jack?" Sheriff Bill Twisdell was already thinking of any others who might have a disliking for Mabry, who was a man well-known as stuck in his ways and beliefs. "We'll take a poke out that way in the mornin' and look around. Might find somethin' interestin'."

The pair was at the site in the early morning when the sun was introducing itself again, touching the shadows, the shapes in shadows and the shapes making the shadows, the long shadows getting shorter, the short shadows disappearing quick as bird to wing. Twisdell spent long minutes looking at every mark he noticed, in and out of the shadows. Sometimes the sun made notes for him, places to look at.

At one point he called Mabry to his side. "Look at this, Jack." He was pointing to a mark on a boulder at the foot of a tree. "I'd say that you put a round off this here boulder, and it hit right there." He put his finger on a spot of the curved surface of the boulder. "From this I'd say you figured the backstabber was close around here. If he's stupid enough to do somethin' like this bushwhacking in the first place, he's stupid enough to leave some kind of sign. We just got to find it." He looked up and added, "Course he might go on and try it all over again." He leveled his eyes at Mabry, as if there was a dare in it, but the devoted wrangler never bit the chew offered.

Twisdell continued looking, studying every little patch of ground, tree or rock surface, and found where a bullet must have clipped a few young limbs, allowed sap to flow for a short time, but leaving a track for his keen eyes.

"You fired them five shots all in this area, Jack, so let's go back over it again." Then he said, "How long you been ridin' that horse you're on now, Jack? You sure do take a lot of stock in him. I tell you, some boys talk about that horse of yours, like a jealous bull in the corral."

Mabry smiled and said, "Gone past seven years now, me bein' on Hobo, Bill, and I'll keep him 20 if I can last that long myself. He listens to me and I listen to him. Tells me a lot, he does. Lays his ears flat back on his neck tellin' me he's bothered by what I'm doin' or where we're goin'. When somethin's goin' on around us, like a critter or a stranger, he flicks those ears like he was a scout. When I feed him good or go easy on the proddin', he puts them ears to the day comin' at us, just like he's happy to be workin' with me. And I know pretty darn early when he's sick, or got a belly ache or somethin' like that, like he tells me with them ears, like they're extra tongues talkin' right at me."   "He makes you jump, right, Jack?"

"Yup, like it's his kitchen most of the time, and he's the boss, like my mother was, bless her soul."

Mabry continued to talk, then realized the sheriff obviously knew all the old stuff he was spitting out and was more interested in a sign he'd just found, making his hands fly up in the air, his head start nodding, like he'd just found a gold nugget at his feet and was lost in the quick study of it.

In between two rocks, in soft ground and not hard gravel, as if it had been put there by Mother Nature for surprise growth, but only a few weeds there at struggling, he found a boot print. All the signs were firm, measurable, and brought up images in Twisdell's mind. "Way it sets, heavy-like, says he's a big man, Jack. Lot bigger than Parlee, who ain't much bigger than a boy waitin' to ride a horse for the first time. Know any big men who want you dead quick as thunder?"

"Not that I do, Sheriff. Not yet, but they might be over the hill, around the bend in the trail like you say."

While Mabry was talking, Twisdell's eye caught something else in the ground. "Jack, did you come chasin' in here after the shootin'?"

Didn't do none of that, Bill. Why you askin'?"

"Well, it looks to me that there was two of them critters in here. Found a smaller boot print over here. Two of them for sure. A big man and a smaller man, or a tall man and a little man with a foot like a boy's. Know anyone like that hangin' out together? I sure don't, but now we got a sign or two to keep to mind."

"Funny pair for a match-up, Bill, how big and little get throwed together for a bushwhackin'."

"Hey, Jack, my daddy used to say all the time, tryin' to give me his best advice and countin' on me listenin', 'Fools go on fool errands with other fools.'"

The event and the situation was squeezed down to a thing of the past, and life for Mabry the wrangler went on its working manner, until one of the cowpokes said one evening as he came back from a visit to his sister down-trail a dozen miles, "You was sayin', Jack, about the big guy with a little guy."

"I did say that a time or two," Mabry said, "Why'd you spit it out now?"

"Down in Holbrook, just a few days ago, I saw a pair look like you said. One guy bigger'n a horse with his pard I first noticed 'cause he was sittin' down and wearin' boots so small I don't know how they made them, except for little kids and not for workin' a horse all day long. Tiniest feet I ever saw and mounted with spurs, mind you like they was too big for them little boots. Then this big guy stands up first and the little one and it's like a circus show, the pair of them walkin' out like they was goin' to do an act with the clowns in the carnie. There was a few laughs, but kind of covered up over 'cause that big guy is as mean lookin' as he is big."

"Do you know who they are?" Mabry said. "Any names?
68

Workin' on a spread some place down that way?"

"One gent I heard say somethin' about them workin' at the Foxtrot spread, over in Galena, next town down to the river not more'n five miles or so."

An hour later, when Bill Twisdell showed up at his office, Mabry told him about the two cowpokes working for the Foxtrot spread. "Big and little, just like you figured, Bill. You had them pegged on the button. How do we handle this? "

"You don't, Jack. I'll poke into this, look them up. Ask questions. My way. We got no connection to Parlee from where we're sittin' now. None at all from where I'm lookin'. You just take care of your horses and I'll do the sheriffin'."

Twisdell was a couple of miles out of town, on his way to check out the suspect pair, when he noticed, for the second time, that a rider was behind him, keeping pace. He nodded as if he had an audience, figuring the rider behind him to be a true lover of horses, Jack Mabry. He pulled his horse into small copse of trees and waited.

When he stepped out in front of Mabry, Mabry was not surprised at all and said, "I knowed you was someplace in there, Bill, because old Hobo here just told me to clear my eyes and keep alert. I'm just figurin' to lend a hand case you might need it."

They rode on as a tandem, idle chatter covering the time, watching the beginning of a drive starting to head up far across the range, a hawk make a kill not far from them and lifting off with a jack rabbit of good size, the scatter of prairie dogs at quick moments, until they saw the marker for the Foxtrot spread, a small, carved sign of good letters and one arrow pointing the way.

Twisdell, wearing his badge shining like a real star, rode right up to the decent-sized ranch house and a man and woman setting the porch at real relaxing.

"The woman looked up, smiled at the badge and kept on with hand work with needles. The man, in his late forties, happy-faced like he was pleased to see visitors, stood up, looked at Twisdell's badge, and said, "Can I help you with something, Sheriff? This is my spread, the Foxtrot. This is my wife Mirabelle and I'm Sandy Hooks."

Twisdell tipped his cap and said, "Ma'am," soft but clear, and

69

looked back at Hooks. "I'm Sheriff Bill Twisdell from Chapstown up the trail, and this here gent is Jack Mabry, a wrangler from one of our spreads back that way, and he was near bushwhacked by two men back a bit. We had an idea about things that bring us to your place."

Hooks said, "That so?" and looked at Mabry and said, "Well, sir, I guess they was tryin' to steal that horse off'n you. I'd settle for a few of him around here. That is some animal. Yes, sir, some animal. I spotted him before I spotted you, course I ain't slightin' you any, mister, 'cause you're ridin' somethin' special I could see all the way in here."

Mirabelle Hooks was smiling at her husband as he spoke, though her fingers kept at their business.

Twisdell said, "What brings us here is a pair of dudes that travel together, a real big man and a pard that might be half his size. You have anybody like that in your bunkhouse?" And as if to prevent a lie or a cover-up from starting, he added, "We had a gent tell us somethin' that brings us right here."

Mrs. Hooks looked at her husband, her hands ceasing their work, the look saying to Twisdell, "Now don't you do any lyin', Sandy."

"Strange you say that, Sheriff. We got a pair exactly like that, but I ain't seen Big Boy all day. Fact is, I ain't seen him since maybe noon yesterday. That's Big Boy Benson I'm talkin' about, one of my hands, a mean one at times I might add but his daddy and momma was good friends of mine and he gets some slack from me, but only some. He does have a mean streak in him. The other fella, Pippy, Pippy Andrews, a little Scotsman. is his regular pard, and scared to death of Big Boy but uses him as a guard of sorts, like you know what I mean."

"This Pippy, is he around now?" Twisdell looked out over a ranch area neat as a beehive, maintenance and care evident in all the parts, the ranch house itself, fence posts and rails, corrals, a low-slung bunkhouse with one dormer, a major-size barn and two smaller barns, and two outhouses on opposites ends of the ranch house area.

"He certainly is," Mrs. Hooks said, I saw him not an hour ago and he was going into the bunkhouse. He hasn't ridden out yet that I've seen." She went back to her needles after smiling an apology to her husband for beating him to the punch, telling on an employee

70

before her husband had to.

Hooks said, "Let's go see what he has to say about any of this. He might know where Big Boy is." Hooks started off to the bunkhouse with Twisdell and Mabry behind him. He walked with a steady gait, with purpose.

Pippy Andrews was smaller than Twisdell or Mabry had even pictured, much a boy as anything except for a sort of wizened, aged face of a 40-year old man, eyes narrowly apart, mouth small, and ears tight to his head. Small but sudden jerks of nervousness quickly took over him as he saw Twisdell's badge and Hooks right behind him. It appeared he had no recognition of Mabry.

Hooks said, "Pippy, where's Big Boy? We ain't seen him since yesterday."

"I know why you're here," Andrews said, his whole little body all aquiver by this time, the little boots, like toys, shaking on his feet.

"What's that, Pippy?" Twisdell said. "Why are we here?"

Pippy Andrews, all as though the hanging shadows were coming down over him, said, "Parlee did it. Said we could have your horse if we got you. Said your horse is the best around. He knowed that all along." He died saying that. Big Boy killed him when we said we missed killin' that fella with the great horse. He's down in a copse near the small bend in the river. Maybe the buzzards got him by now or the coyotes."

He still didn't recognize Mabry. "Then Big Boy tried to say he was going to keep the horse for himself, that I was a shrimp of a man, a boy of a man, and couldn't handle that horse, so I shot him, the big mouth. He's always the big mouth and I just wanted to get up on that horse like I was king of the grass and ride him all day long. That horse could ride me forever, any place I wanted to go. I know it."

"Where's Big Boy now?" Hooks said.

"Right where we left Parlee, in them trees." He was standing, and looked out the bunkhouse window and saw Hobo tied to the rail of the ranch house.

It must have all dawned on him at that moment and he looked at Mabry and said, "Is that your horse, mister? Is it really yours? Are you the fella Big Boy shot at?"

He shook his head in wonder and awe, other resolutions dawning on him, and then he looked at Hobo again and said, "I just

71

wanted to ride him all day on the grass, mister. Just one day all by myself and nobody, not even big mouth Big Boy sayin' a word to me 'cause they couldn't catch up to me, me and your horse. Just one day."

He closed his eyes, his little frame shaking all over, waiting for whatever came next, knowing that he had lost out on the ride of his life.

Garcy Pewter, owner of the small Box B spread, squeezed himself into a ball, pulled his legs up as tight as he could, and held his breath. He could smell the moisture on his body. If the Indians with their keen sense of smell found him, he didn't know how long he'd last. "They have ways," he kept hearing from all the old timers of the area, and they always raised their eyebrows when they made that statement. He was on a ledge under an overhang in the canyon. His horse was dead on the floor of the canyon after the fall, ready to feed whatever animals fed on dead horsemeat. The bullet had missed him by inches, but the horse was not so lucky. When the old gray went down, Pewter was hanging on to the reins, and was able to swing inward and land on the ledge. The horse kept going. Pewter never heard him hit the bottom.

He had other things on his mind, which tried to wrap around the whole scene, measuring as he always did. When he shook his head at the implausibility of his situation, he said, "I don't know where you are, Lord, but I hope you're near and listening to me."

In the first place, he remembered, there had been his foray into the hills above Noshegan, a small town in southern Idaho. It was stupid to go alone, he was admitting, for the renegades were all around, stealing, kidnapping, and causing misery. But he was too damned rambunctious to sit still and wait for justice … and justice is what his soul clamored for.

He had been plain mad for a week. His best horses were taken in the raid on the Box B, the two swaybacks and the mules left behind, as if to say they couldn't be bothered with trash animals. On the ledge, fearful of capture, he was still mad, even as he heard them passing overhead, talking in a language he didn't understand. Not a word of it. Except a kind of wild threat seemed to be cast about. His interpretation made him reach to see if his side arms were still in their holsters. Moving his hands as slowly as possible, he reached to see if he was armed. The sigh of relief almost escaped from him in a rush as he found the Colts still in place. It was a miracle. "Yes," he said, "a miracle of good leather-making."

The morning came back to him as vivid as a painting; he cresting the hill above the ranch house and seeing the raid in progress, the corral gate lowered and two Indians were driving the

73

horses out of the corral. Another brave made sure the swaybacks and the mules stayed where they were. From where Pewter was, a hundred yards away, he began firing at them. They fled with his horses.

His two ranch hands, he figured, had been drawn off on a ruse so they would not deter the horses being stolen. He guessed his help to be up the canyon a ways and would be rushing back at the sound of the gunfire. They did not come back to check on the ranch or the stock, or him. That bothered him. He'd have to check, hoping they were holed up someplace, still in one piece. He closed the gate at the corral and the door to the barn. Two of his large pigs were loose at the back of the barn and he brought them back to the pen with a heavy share of grain mix.

Anger could well be tempered by hard work, expending energy, he told himself, but that argument was raising other arguments.

With anxiety building inside him, he went looking for his ranch hands in the north pastures. They were good old boys who had been with him for a few years, the pair of them good with guns, courage and each one carried a good deal of horse sense. Yet he suspected they had been drawn to the north quarter by a bogus raid.

Nothing was moving in the broad sweep of his view: no cows, no horses, and no cowboys. His nerves belted him with a new onslaught. He hungered for fairness, for chance, for the yield of long hard hours of work, for the safety of his two ranch hands.

Pewter knew he was continually caught up in arguments within himself. Life was rife with such dictates: good horse or bad horse, good gun or bad gun, good worker or bad worker, good Indian or bad Indian, good idea or bad idea, good feeling or bad feeling. Life came with choice, options, chance. He wondered, had he misplaced something along the way?

"Lord," he muttered, almost so he wouldn't hear his own voice, "I hope you keep me and the boys company."

Even as he spoke, the quandary seemed to follow him, ride in the same saddle with him, and hang on him sure as leather.

Overhead the sun moved in a slow arc from its morning introduction, heading to the Rockies in the far west. A wide-winged hawk rode a thermal in a bright scrap of sky and a coyote called for attention in one of the ravines. In the air he caught an unknown

74

aroma and thought of the adventures that came to a man in newness, in something as minimal as an odor on the air. In a perfect world he could enjoy all that bloomed around him ... sound, beauty, essence of some order he vaguely understood as belonging to a man who cared.

That reverie shook him awake.

If his boys were not visible, "not dead" he said half aloud, they had to be hidden somewhere along the cliff line. He fired a shot and called their names, cupping his mouth as he called out. Holding the reins in place, to still his mount, he listened for any reply. All remained quiet, the silent hawk, the coyote for the while, his ranch hands wherever he hoped they had hidden from the raiding Indians that had run off his horses, the good ones.

He called again, fired another shot. Heard nothing.

In a few moments tracks showed in the grass when he crossed them, leading to the steep climb to the tree level. Then faces of his ranch hands, Smithburg and Stallings, lit the back of him mind with smiles. He said another prayer, for he had heard nothing in response to his signals, his cries. As he crowned a lip of a sudden wadi he saw two horses dead on the slight downhill slope. He saw no ranch hands. No bodies. No signs of a struggle except for the dead horses.

Then, from a distance, from higher than his level, came a slight flash, a reflection off the edge of the tree line. He froze in his seat. If it was an Indian with a rifle he might be aiming at him now, but he had to assume one Indian would not fire at him, not give away his hiding place; the trade-off was not good enough.

On the other hand, if it was one of his boys, it could be a signal that there was someone in the way of rescue. He thought over carefully the new set of options, enemy or friend making a signal; an Indian inadvertently causing a reflection, one of his ranch hands sending a warning that he should not ignore for one moment. Life was full of options, choices, opportunities, and the endless quandaries.

The flash came again. Then again. Moving a few paces he found it stopped. He went back to where he was, and the signal came again. He had to be in the line of sight of the sender who had to be in the edges of the tree line. So, he guessed, an enemy had to be hidden between the two points.

Pewter slipped out of the saddle, hobbled his horse to a clump of bush, rubbed his neck to gentle him, and crawled forward. He went past the dead horses, saw the blood flow on the grass, and saw tracks heading to the woods. He circled to his right, keeping an eye on the ground between him and the point where the signal had been sent.

No movement caught his eye, but he saw an Indian brave behind a stump, still, as if he was protecting himself from gunfire from up the hill. Pewter, putting his rifle sight on the back of the brave, wanting to squeeze off a round, found himself locked into another situation … the brave did not seem to move at all, as if he was dead already. He eased off the trigger and watched. The Indian did not move, not a muscle. Pewter studied him, wondered how old he was, did he have a wife, or children. How many scalps were hung on his teepee pole? Why didn't he move? Could other than a dead man stay so still?

Pewter aimed at the stump, at the demand of something inside him. He squeezed the trigger, and fired the round. The slug hit the stump and the Indian did not move. He must be dead, Pewter thought. He rose slowly and walked toward the Indian leaning against the stump. The brave was dead, his mouth open wide, his eyes closed as if in prayer. He looked to be in his mid-thirties, had large hands, good-sized arms, a thick mass of black hair, paint on his face, and blood on his chest. An amulet of some sort he wore around his neck. It was not made of teeth. Pewter had no idea what it was, but he took the amulet as a souvenir or a sign of conquest. Some good horses he had lost this day. He was not sure about his men. One of his men must have killed the brave. He put the amulet around his own neck.

A voice called from uphill. "Hey, Boss, I been hit. Stallings, too. He might be dead or real bad off, Boss. He's in another hole near me, but I can't get to him. I'm glad you saw the reflections. That bozo down there has had us pinned down for a few hours. Did you get him with that one shot?"

Pewter replied, "I think you got him, Smitty. He was dead already. I'm coming up."

They brought Stallings home across the saddle behind Smithburg. Pewter walked the whole way, leading the horse.

At the Box B, Smitty's wounds tended, Pewter asked, "How many were up there with you?"

76

"Just the one. I didn't see any others."

Pewter said, "I saw only two down here, so it was a small party using their numbers best they could. They got my best horses. I'm going after them."

"I wish I could go with you, Boss, but I'd only drag on you."

"You just keep a keen eye out here at the ranch. I'll be back tomorrow, or the next day. If I don't get back, you got yourself a new ranch. I'll sign a paper to that effect. If I don't do something now, they'll only come back again, us being a soft touch for them." His voice changed. "It ain't gonna be that way."

He rode off on the one good horse left on his ranch.

Which was now dead more than 100 feet below him.

Pewter was fit to be tied, but mostly mad at himself for being so exposed, being a soft touch for a small group of Indians. He suspected they were a minor renegade party, but had a smart leader.

He moved his arms and legs, arched his back, wanted to make sure he was able to do something to protect himself, try to get his horses back. A man without horses was lost out here. In the back end of a canyon he finally had seen them, and his horses. Three braves were sharing food, while a fourth one kept the horses tightly in against the canyon wall, holding them in a make-shift corral of brambles, brush and a few branches.

From the top of the trail he had spotted them as he moved warily along an old pathway. None of them, he thought, had seen him, but the round had come from somewhere else, from another brave on lookout, perhaps, or a new arrival.

But his last horse was gone. And he was lucky. He cursed the anger that had driven him to come this far alone.

Pewter got to his feet, shaking and shivering in his bones, afraid of falling off the edge. He had to get to a point of maneuvering, get an edge back that was lost for a couple of days. Along the wall the ledge was wide enough to shuffle as long as he held on with a tight grip. How long before they spotted him he had no idea, but it wouldn't be long. For thirty or so feet he moved on the ledge until he saw a cleft he could slide into.

He slipped inside the crevice. It widened, had more room overhead, allowed him to stand fully upright and promised even a bigger opening further on. It was a cave he had entered. No growls came, or hisses, no animal sounded out its possession of the cave. It

77

was dark but Pewter felt around him the tumble of stones and boulders. With lots of effort, he blocked the way behind him with good-sized rocks; there was no way he could let himself be captured. If an exit came up ahead of him, a getaway loomed possible. His guns were at his side; all he needed was one horse to get home. Yeh, one horse loose on the mountain. Chance, choice, opportunity might not come along so often. The questions and the doubts came from every direction.

In some manner his anger began to slip away from him. He thought the anger must be dissipated by the adventure ahead of him. The grasp for continued life.

So he thought.

At the end of the cave, as it narrowed down to a small opening allowing him to slip through, Pewter felt a cool freshet of air circulated around him. Outside the cave he saw, below him, a small valley covered with green grass, a small waterfall about a hundred yards away, three Indians sitting by fire, and a bunch of horses tied to a loose line. He wondered if any of them were his.

Well, he thought, I've come this far. Might as well find out. He looked around him for a way down. The one certain belief he had was that he had to get onto a horse. He was lost without a horse. He wished he had his rifle, but that was with his horse at the bottom of the canyon behind him.

Off to the left was a jagged line against the cliff face, and it angled down to the floor of the valley. Most likely an old trail he surmised. "Downward, and onward," he said to himself, and made his way as soundless as he could, moving very slowly, often immobile. He kept his eyes on the Indians who stared into the fire. Around a tall stone pillar he went, out of sight of the Indians, and came onto ground level after a slow and clumsy descent. A horse snickered. Guttural speech of one brave came to his ears. Meat of some kind was cooking, and the aroma was delicious.

A horse snickered again. A pebble fell onto a stone, the faint sound alarming. He meant to turn, but his arms were suddenly pinned by arms stronger than his own. He smelled the breath of the Indian who embraced him from behind and who was hooting and hollering as loud as possible. The braves at the fire sprang to help horse collar him further. They tied him tightly and dragged him to the fire, laughing all the way, their faces painted, their movements

78

menacing, their cries nothing but jubilation.

He swore he blacked out. It might have been from the surprise, the rough handling, the leather binds tight all over his body, breathing at times as hard as if a horse kicked him. When he was fully conscious, Garcy Pewter found himself tied between two rugged saplings, with his arms extended and parallel to the ground. Dryness scoured his throat.

The noise at the campfire was on-going, with a great dash of vengeance in it. He agreed that that determination was a liberal choice of his own … many Indians were due for justice, but this particular group probably didn't qualify. He had one dead ranch hand and some missing horses to find, scores to settle.

Once in a while one of the braves would walk past him and jab him with a stick or throw water at his feet but never in his face. For the first time Pewter realized Indians laughed like some of his pals in a saloon on Saturday night. His captives laughed continually, one of them pointing out and obviously counting the horses in the make-shift corral. An education was coming at him and he took it all in.

One of them laughed and threw more water on his boots when Pewter said, "Do you believe in the same God I do?" Laughter and understanding did not seem to go together. "Why do you throw water at my feet and not at my mouth?" There was more laughter and he was sure none of them understand his words.

He passed out a couple of times. Each time he came to he could feel pains all over his body, not sure how they had been delivered to him.

This last time he remembered they started using sticks on him, slashing and beating him and poking him where it really hurt. He could only cry out. It went on for hours at a time, then they'd eat and work on the horses and gather firewood and one or another would come back from hunting with a rabbit or a bird. No big game. They cooked, ate, laughed, and then began hurting him again

None of the food was offered to him. The beatings did not stop. The laughter did not stop, and the wild language they used.

Pewter called on his God as often as he could, as loud as he could. One of the Indians jabbed him with his stick and tore his shirt. He laughed at that and was about to jab him again when he screamed out and fell to his knees. Pewter remembered that moment ever afterward. Chance. Choice. Opportunity. God at hand.

The other braves rushed from the campfire and the Indian torturing Pewter yammered again and pointed at Pewter. He was almost hysterical.

The others stared with open-mouths at the amulet hanging on Pewter's neck. One of them seemed to be hypnotized and stayed on his knees for a long while. When he rose he went to the small corral and broke down a part of the barrier, tossing limbs and brush aside. The horses drifted out through the break, a few at first, and then all of them after he hollered loudly and waved them out. In a smooth move, attesting to horse experience, the Indian roped one horse and brought it to the campfire.

All the Indians fell to their knees, talking and yacking and yammering one atop the other, and then all together, as if in a chorus, they chanted one word in their language. It sounded like 'Wakatanka' to Pewter who did not understand the word.

And they kept looking up at the sky.

But everything had changed. God, who was around, had answered.

An ax swung in the air, cutting the leather binds on one tree, and then it bit into the other tree. Pewter's arms fell like rocks. Two of the braves caught him as he fell and brought him to the campfire, looking overhead all the time. Water was given to him from a gourd, a little at a time, and then he was given some cooked meat that he ate ravenously. More jabbering went on between the Indians and one by one, in sudden silence, each of the braves touched the amulet still sitting on Pewter's chest.

The horse brought to the campfire was one of Pewter's mares, a rugged gray, and one brave hung a gourd on Pewter's shoulder and three of them hoisted him up on the horse. The braves stared into the sky as they put him up on the horse. They all stood back as one young brave pointed the way out, where the horses, a dozen of them, were drifting off.

Bareback, clutching the horse's mane, Pewter nudged the horse forward. The big gray, with a known weight on its back, caught up with the freed horses. Pewter yelled them on and waved his arms and all the horses went into a quick trot and headed to the pass that lead to the great prairie beyond.

Pewter did not look back, glad to be out of there, to be on the move, to be on a horse, to have his horses back. He kept thinking of the sudden change in the Indians, realizing the amulet he had taken from the dead Indian had some kind of power over them, or which they held in some kind of reverence. None of the other Indians wore such an amulet, he had checked that out as they had set him up on the gray.

Why had that one Indian, driving Smitty and Stallings to cover, killing Stallings, getting killed by either one of them, been alone at his end of the raid? Pewter figured he had been alone, as he had seen only the four others in the camp, including the one that had caught him coming down the trail. He also assumed the Indians believed he had killed the brave who wore the amulet he now had on his own chest.

He touched his hand to it and felt nothing. When he looked down at it extended onto his hand by its leather string, he noted it was not a tooth, not a piece of bone or a piece of wood, but a piece of odd stone in a strange shape. He saw or smelled nothing from the piece of stone.

But something touched him.

The first actual thought that came at him was the many stories of stray stars or pieces of stone that had come out of night skies bound for Earth. Mountain men and trappers and night riders of cattle herds and late customers in saloons had often spoken of streaks of fire falling from the skies to any place beyond them, in the mountain or out on the wide grass. Few of those who saw such sights had time to chase down the places where the objects had hit and burrowed into the land. Now and then, some Indian must have followed the arrow of fire hitting the earth, perhaps quite near him.

He wondered about the piece of stone, an odd stone he agreed, that he now wore hanging on his neck. When he got settled down again, he'd go looking for plausible answers. His rescue deserved some explanation, but he didn't know where to start.

In a day's work he managed to get the horses back to his spread and into a corral. Smitty was up and about, and had taken care of Stallings and his burial. He said, on greeting him, "Boss, I thought I had seen the last of you and might be a new ranch owner, but no such luck."

They both had a hearty laugh over it, and laughed again over dinner after all their work was done for the day.

After Pewter had told the whole story of his time in the secret valley, Smitty said, "Boss, I heard once way back, from that old buck Indian who camps way out on Luke Jurgen's spread, that something fell out of the sky one night when he was a tyke. He said the moon was bright and then went behind a cloud and things got scary, and it was like a falling star coming across the whole world, silent but red as fire. Damned thing, whatever it was, suddenly came down, and went right through the hands of an old sachem who was asking for a sign from the gods. The old sachem, without a cry of pain, stood and said one word, 'Wakatanka.'"

Smitty finished his tale. "That was the end of his story. I never heard the word again from him, or the old buck would never tell me again. Spooky stuff if you ask me. Wakatanka."

Pewter, something suddenly clicking in his mind, jumped at the word from Smitty's mouth. "That's what the Indians said up there in that valley, 'Wakatanka.' I'm sure of it. Sure as hell."

"That's a strange testament to heaven," Smitty said. "We better go see that old buck one day soon."

With such knowledge at hand, Pewter could not delay his visit to the old Indian. In the morning he and Smitty were on their way to Luke Jurgen's spread. It was up-range about a dozen miles. They arrived after an easy ride and Smitty pointed out an old shack up against a sharp-rising cliff.

"That's where he lives, Boss. His name is Slow Dog and Luke lets him stay here. Says his whole tribe is almost gone from the area now. Only a few of them around. He's a Cherokee. Once he was the shaman for them." He helloed the shack and the old Indian came out.

Slow Dog was about 85 years old, blind in one eye, few teeth left, but carried himself with a confident grace. The smile across his face was authentic, and he held out both of his hands, one for Smitty and one for Pewter, and he pointed at a sitting log in front of the shack. An Indian woman, much younger, carried out a pipe and gave it to the old one, and set down a board with three mugs on it.

They sat on the log and sipped a rare kind of tea. The wind was mute. The sun was almost straight overhead. Peace was spread far and wide by silence.

Pewter remembered the other Indians and how they stared at the sky. Something else clicked in his mind and he reached inside his shirt and pulled out the stone amulet. He held it up for Slow Dog to see.

With one hand held like a visor over his good eye, Slow Dog looked overhead, seeing where the sun was. Tremors shook him visibly and he said, "You must go quick before the sun gets long and throws your shadow on me. Do not throw your shadow on me. I am too old and only have a few days to feel the wind and to stick my hands in the earth. Do not throw your shadow on me." He was pointing at Pewter. "Wakatanka watches. Wakatanka listens. Wakatanka waits for his shadow to catch up to him. Do not throw your shadow on me. I have seen the stone from the skies that calls for men in the shadows."

Pewter, understanding all that had happened to him, around him, knew that God, by whatever name he was called, had made an appearance. And Slow Dog, the last shaman of the Cherokee, knew what would bring him down from the skies and make new demands in the shadows.

Gaucho from Chestnut Hill

He came west from Boston-town and carried his own bit of history with him, that history being varied, complex, and somewhat international.

For much of the early years of his life, perhaps from 4 to 12 years, Chadsey Brenault Cushing dreamed of someone being nearly strangled by a flying bola, thrown from the hands of a South American Gaucho. He didn't know the name of the victim, but he hoped it wasn't himself in such dire straits. From his first days of listening to stories at the knee of his grandfather, to the day he started reading entirely on his own, in a large house on the Newton-Boston line, in Chestnut Hill, Chadsey Brenault Cushing was in love with the cowboys of South America and their talent with that favorite weapon. Bolas were weights encased in skins attached to ropes of a sort, and could be one or two or three weights tied together. Escape by an animal, or a man, on the Pampas was often doomed by skilled bola throwers.

"The bola," he'd often say in his made-up games of pretense, "is my weapon of choice." He had heard himself say that so many times, it sat there at the corner of his mouth waiting to be said again:

"The bola is my weapon of choice."

The Bola Perdida or Bola Loca, (Crazy or Lost Ball), had one ball and it became his first choice of bolas that included "Avestrucera or nanducera" with 2 weights; "Boleadora or Tres Marias or Tres Potreadoras" that countered with 3 weights.

Young Cushing discovered, from early history, that the Indians from Las Pampas in South America were the first to develop the bolas and the gauchos or cowboys of South America soon employed them as distinctive weapons for hunting ... and hurting their enemies. The first examples of bolas were usually made of stone, with the weights encased in fresh leather that shrank as a tight cover of the heavy--weighted weapon.

His grandfather, knowing some treatment was needed to alleviate the boy's bad dreams, made the first bola for young Chadsey. In fact, he made a succession of them for the boy, and moved him right past his fright and into a total obsession with the bola weapon and its place in history.

84

The elder Cushing, once a stowaway on a black ship from Ireland, who rose to prominence in the whaling and shipping business, not only made the first bolas for his grandson, but taught him how to use them. He had learned from runaway gauchos that had made their way to the open seas, much the way he had escaped hungry Ireland, land of famine and loss.

By the time he was 15, an expert in using the bola, and carrying a fever and hunger in his gut for moving on from Boston and its tamed atmosphere, he decided to go west. He did not have the slightest desire to follow his father into the whaling business, a fact known by his grandfather but not his father.

And young Cushing had no desire to go to South America either: Texas was far enough for him. He had wheat-colored hair, usually unkempt, very little flair for the niceties of the region he grew up in, loved stories about "other places around the Earth," and harbored dreams anew about excitements that lay ahead of him in this life.

On May Day, 1866, the Great War over, though troubles persisted on many borders, Chad Cushing left Missouri as a member of a wagon train under the command of Barnard "Barnie" Woolcomb, a man of prodigious size and strength who often rode a Percheron mount, now and then a Clydesdale, each one from his own remuda attached to the wagon train. Woolcomb was a fearful sight in the saddle.

Once seeing young Cushing practicing with a bola, Woolcomb questioned him about its use at length, asked for additional displays of dexterity from Cushing, and assigned him as an outside guard and lookout, giving the youngster special instructions.

"Listen carefully, Chad," he advised the youngster, "I've been this way a few times and always had trouble of some sort from a small but inventive gang who use different ways to steal from us. We've never been able to catch even one of them. Shot a couple dead, right in the saddle, but never got any information from the dead. Do you think, with that wild thing you swing about, you might stop a man or his horse in their tracks? Enough so we can go raid their hideout, wherever it is? Their territory's coming up in a day or two, however the weather takes us, or the winds, you name it. We're lucky the big river's behind us."

For the next two days, exhibiting all the caution he could bring to a new job, Cushing continually remembered what his grandfather had said about being prepared for all things. Not once did he scramble his silhouette across a skyline, keeping him and his horse in lower extremes, in the wadis and gullies and low spots in the grass, or behind boulders and odd rocks and trees in small or large clusters.

With his eyes wide open all the time for slight movements, Cushing was adamant that he could see a speck moving on the horizon.

It was early on day three, the sun splayed like a torch on the grass, his horse Bunker Hill steady as a rocky outcrop under him, he saw a flicker of movement on a skyline that merged rock and trees around a stretch of grass. The movement of a horse and rider, with its slow gait and direction, told Cushing where he'd meet it. He rode Bunker Hill down into a wadi, then into a small canyon he had traveled the day before, and came out well ahead of the rider, near two large trees about 60 feet apart.

The rider was obviously being cautious about his movements, keeping to shadows when he could, staying off the skyline, the same maneuvers Cushing had used himself.

In a brief shadow from an overhanging cliff, the rider positioned himself and his horse in the heart of the shadow, about 200 yards away from the trees where Cushing watched him. To Cushing the rider was obviously set to spy on the wagon train for the legendary gang that Woolcomb had talked about.

Cushing began to consider the full understanding of his task, so he studied the spy, as he called him, as best he could; the size of the man, the type of horse, and determining the weapons he carried. Obvious to him were the twin hand guns at the man's waist and what looked like a rifle in a saddle scabbard. The man seemed to be a definite counterpart to Cushing himself; young, doing his best to remain hidden.

Who and what that other man was and where he fit into things became affixed in Cushing's mind, which was why he was out here in the first place.

That was his task … to undertake and carry off as best he could. For the young Bostonian transplanted into a new life, this was a huge initiation to endure. His focus kept hold of the important observations that he'd already found out.

Now and then the spy rider's horse, looking like a chestnut in color, shifted his weight, nickered with an echo off the rock surface, but remained in place, like a well-trained animal. Cushing was glad the slight breeze was coming at him from the shadowed rider, for Bunker Hill twitched his ears and Cushing knew he had caught scent of the other pair.

If he could get the other man to ride away, perhaps in a sprint and not catching sight of Cushing for a short period, he'd have a decent chance of stopping his flight. The bola was comfortable in Cushing's hands, Bunker Hill would do as prompted, and the new assignment might be completed.

"Presence of mind," came back to him, as he heard his grandfather's voice say for seemingly the thousandth time. "Presence of mind and a plan without quit in it."

A procession of order came out of his mind, "Came up for air," as his grandfather might have said.

It made him grind away at the mix of knowledge he'd come into, conceive a plan, and set about to complete it. With Bunker Hill off a ways from his position, he gathered a few small branches, found one round stone, dug out a piece of jerky from his shirt pocket, and set his plan into operation. The stone, a round one, sat atop a miniature tepee-like structure he had set up, with the jerky on top of the stone. It would not take long for its scent to be picked up; he had already heard small animals moving near him.

Silently Cushing went off to get Bunker Hill, disappeared down a dip in the grass, and then into a deep wadi. With shadows beginning to spawn from high places, and able to move slowly within the shadows, he was soon beyond the other rider, still sitting hopefully in the same place, merged against the rock face.

Cushing had a good idea that the rider, if surprised, would rush back the way he had come. He and the bola would be waiting for him.

A breeze rose in the east and blew across the grass toward the mysterious rider. It carried the scent of the jerky with it, for the horse nickered a few times. Cushing, off behind a rise and another growth of brush by a pile of rocks, did not hear the other horse, but was keeping Bunker Hill as quiet as possible. Cushing felt the breeze behind him and realized the scent of the jerky would be carried along with the breeze.

As Cushing moved closer to the watchful rider still sitting the saddle, from just about where he had come from, he suddenly heard the noise from his jerky-tepee contraption. Some hungry critter, catching scent of the jerky, must have gone after it, broke down the small structure, from which the round stone rolled down the rocky slope. The noise, though not very loud, was distinct, and set the spy rider into flight back the way he had come.

With his horse at a quick gallop, the spy was in hasty flight and might not have seen Cushing swing in behind him, Bunker Hill at a pace with the other horse, the bola twirling over Cushing's head. The spy had no idea what was coming his way, even as he finally noticed Cushing coming up behind him.

The aim of the bola, as if it had eyes in the encased balls, swung through the air in a concentrated arc, a slight hum in its wake, a surprising result coming on the targeted young rider and his horse.

The hoof sounds were drum-like, the whir of the bola like a sibilant music, the quiet prairie alive with flight and desperation in two quarters.

Flight ended quickly, as the spy's horse went foundering with his two front legs tautly enmeshed in rope bindings tough enough to drop him in his tracks. That sudden halt threw the rider head-first over his horse and onto the ground where he lay stunned.

Cushing leaped down from Bunker Hill and tied the rider's hands and feet as quickly as he could. The horse was not hurt by the bola and Cushing tossed the captured man belly-first over his saddle, tied him in place, and set off for the wagon train.

Woolcomb, out front of the wagon train as it started to roll into its nightly protective circle, spotted Cushing and the second horse appear over a rise in the grass. He rode out to meet them.

"What cha got there, Chad? Looks like you been busy a while." He pointed at the man draped over the saddle. "He any part of my discussion a few days ago?"

"He sure is, Mr. Woolcomb, Caught him sitting up in one place where he could watch us as we moved, Could tell a lot about us. How many guns. How many men. Had kind of an idea what they could take from us or run off."

"How'd you know all that, Chad?"

"Oh," Cushing said, "we had a little discussion soon as he woke up from being slightly unconscious when he was toppled right

88

out of his saddle by the gaucho's weapon of choice."

The wide smirk on his face was a joyous one, as if he was saying he was glad he had not gone to sea to become a whaler and settle eventually into the whaling company office.

"What else you find out, Chad, in your little talk?" The smirk was shared by the older wagon master.

"Well, I know they have seven men in their fold. The leader is Black Lester, only name this boy knows him by. They are sitting in a small camp back in those hills out past us, waiting on Jessie's return." He pointed to the other man, "This here's Jessie, Jessie Bowdring, in case you don't know it yet. And he's most willing to join up with us and get away from that wild gang he had to join or get shot."

He paused to get his breath, set the tone, set the command, all the things he had been taught. "We could go up there and drive them right out of the territory, and we won't have to worry about them anymore. Jessie says he can get us right in on top of them. That should take care of this problem, because he says they are bound to go after the next wagon train, and that's us."

Woolcomb said to Jessie, "You up to all that, son?"

"Yes, sir, I am. I was scared all the time I was with 'em. Chad told me it was easier this way, being on the other side, sleepin' better, not worryin' 'bout no sheriff or a posse or stuff like that. Yes, sir, I'm with you and Chad."

"How old are you, Jessie?" Woolcomb said as he began to untie the knots about Jessie's ankles.

"I'm 16, sir. Just turned 16 'bout a month ago."

"Why, you and Chad are just about the same age."

Woolcomb shook his head and said, "Ain't it a wonder how two boys can learn so much in just a couple of days. Ain't that a wonder." He was all smiles as he looked at the two young cowpokes, now under his command.

He looked from Cushing to Jessie and said, "You ever see a bola before, Jessie?" as Cushing put it in Woolcomb's hands.

"No, sir. Never did, and I won't forget this one either. Course, I couldn't explain it to Black Lester either, no matter how hard I tried, and he wouldn't listen no how."

"Oh, he'll hear about it, son. Sure as shootin'."

89

As evening descended on Bartonsville, Texas, smoke and steam issued in cloudy funnels from the Missouri, Kansas, & Texas Railroad Company steam engine and was quickly absorbed by dusk. In the shadows cast by one passenger car, a man stood still and alone, a small night bag in one hand, his other hand close to a revolver holstered on his belt, under his coat. He stared up the tracks toward the engine puffing away in place, and waited in the darkest spot, hidden from all eyes.

The man nobody had seen as yet, including the station ticket seller, grasped a handrail and stepped up to one of the three passenger cars of the train. He was still on the outside platform of the passenger car when the train whistle blew, steam puffed anew, and the wheels began their slow roll into start-up motion.

In the same car, at the far end, in window seat, a young boy, about 8 years of age, sat with his small suitcase, as if there was no way he'd put it out of his sight. Blond hair stood tall on part of his head, the way the wind might blow it unkempt and loose. The pale green shirt he wore and the dark pants were customary attire for a youngster of the area, where cows roamed on all the land and ran loose until they met fence wire or until they stopped for water or by water. The mystery man settled into a seat two rows behind the youngster.

Only a dozen people were in the car, seven women gabbing away at one end, three older men, and the boy and the strange man both sitting by themselves.

The conductor walked up to the boy and said, "You enjoying the ride, son? I got word from your grandfather back there at Washaw to keep my eye on you until we get to Simpson Springs. Only two more stops and you're home with momma's cooking again."

The boy looked up and said, "My mother's sick. She don't cook anymore. She hardly eats either."

The conductor said, "I guess I knew some of that, but not how bad she was. Your grandfather told me she was sick, but not about not eating or cooking. I'm sorry to hear that."

"Pa sent me to visit for a while, but I'll be glad to get back home, see my mother, my father, my horse Flash."

"He quick, son, like his name?"

"Yup," the boy said with a big smile.

When the conductor walked by the stranger, he shrugged his shoulders. The gesture was understood to be about the boy's situation. The stranger nodded, got up and walked to the boy and said, "Son, you ever see the flashing stars of Mount Kilso? They're on our way. They are something else to see. There's a better view from the platform. You interested? I heard you say your horse's name was Flash. From that I guessed you'd be real interested in seeing the flashing stars."

"Sure," the boy said. "Can I leave my bag here?"

"Of course. Nobody's going to steal it. There's no place to go. I even left mine back there." He pointed at his bag sitting on end by his seat, looked around the car at the ladies gabbing, the older men near dozing off, the conductor making his way to the next car.

The two were on the platform for just about two minutes when the man said, "We can get a better look over this side. You have to look up to the north side of Mount Kilso, and keep your eyes open."

When the man jumped off the train, the boy in his arms, there was no sound. No motion. Nobody missed them for over half an hour when the conductor came back and asked the ladies and the old men where the boy was.

One woman said, "He went back there with that man who was sitting behind him. I heard him say they were going to look at the flashing stars."

The conductor hastened to the back of the car, saw nobody and knew his first fear. The boy was the son of the biggest rancher in the area, Jesse Randolph Phillips of the JRP spread that went all the way to the mountains, and then some. They were sixty miles from the boy's destination. At the next stop he sent a telegraph.

The telegraph was delivered to Phillips, and a half a day later one of his horses, wearing his brand, stolen weeks earlier, came back to the JRP ranch lead by a cowboy. "Found him out on the grass, Jesse, and he had this note on him, stuck to the saddle."

The note said, "I got your boy, Phillips. Now it's my turn."

"Who'd write that, Jesse? Who'd take a kid?"

"Someone who hates me, I'd guess, and there's been enough of them; quitters, soreheads, lousy drovers who never pulled their own weight. I can't name one, but can name all of them if needed."

91

He looked at the telegraph sent by the conductor. "Your boy disappeared off the train with a strange man, near Mount Kilso and before we got to Wilson Wells, where I sent this message. The man was in his 40s, bearded, wore a gray hat and a black band on it, black vest, and gray shirt. Carried one pistol with a walnut handle on his belt. Left a bag with nothing in it."

Phillips did not want to tell his wife, who he thought would have died before the boy got back home. Now it looked to be a correct assumption on his part. He called one of his hands and said, "Bliss, go out there on that last round-up at Smoke Ridge and tell Charlie-Two-Horse I need him in a hurry. A real hurry."

Well after midnight, Phillips heard the hoof beats coming down the trail. He knew it was Charlie-Two-Horse, his Apache friend who saved him from Comanches a long time in the past.

The two sat in the kitchen. Phillips said, "Charlie, someone grabbed Jordan off the train. Must have jumped off near Mount Kilso and before Wilson Wells. One of my own horses was brought in by a drover who found him with a note on him, saying they stole the boy and 'It was his turn now.'"

"You don't know who?" Charlie-Two-Horse said.

"Could be one of many, Charlie. But he'll come looking for something else. With Mabel sick these past few years, you had as much to do with bringing Jordan up as anybody. The boy's smart enough to keep his wits about him. You agree?"

"The boy listen all the time. He know many way including the way of the Apache in trouble. He know how to track almost as good as me." He laughed, and said, "Jordan not helpless like man who took him think. He has Apache on his hands. I go now, take two horse. Will look for trail. Do not send army until I look."

Phillips patted him on the back. "Charlie, you've been a great friend, but I need all you have now."

"Charlie know. Jordan know Charlie come. Jordan smart as Apache."

Three miles before Wilson Wells on the railroad, Charlie-Two-Horse found where the two had come off the train and rolled down a grassy embankment, some brush broken and trampling evident on the slope. A mile away, in a grove of trees, he found where two horses had been tied. Tracks lead away in two directions and he knew the first track was light, being rider-less or carrying the boy. But the boy had not turned up, so the horse was rider-less and must have been used to carry the note. The other trail hit rocks and water, and Charlie went all the way back to the jump spot and began to meticulously search the ground, inch by inch, foot by foot.

The smile lit his face up when he found the first bead on the ground, not in grass but on gravel, the sun touching it lightly, the reflection bright. It was a prayer bead from Jordan's holy necklace, the string of beads his grandmother had given him when he was born.

Jordan, part Apache, had started marking his trail.

Walking slowly, leading his horses, Charlie-Two-Horse kept finding the trail of beads. He could picture Jordan snapping them loose one at a time in his pocket, even as he rode doubled-up with the kidnapper.

At one point he found two beads fairly close together and knew the course had been changed. Due north had become due east. More beads showed up. Then two more beads that announced another change in direction.

Charlie-Two-Horse's grin became wider and brighter. The holy beads he did not understand were now telling him what he needed to know.

He travelled all that day, in twists and turns and changes in direction, and finally, as he crested a hill through a scrub growth, he saw the old miner's cabin set against a cliff with a red stone face. He went back a half mile, tied off one horse, and went back to his lookout spot in deep brush. Sitting and waiting in patience, he studied the cabin. The smell of fire in the early morning came with the aroma of coffee. One horse was tied off at the side of the cabin, the saddle sitting on a bench. For a few hours nothing moved outside the cabin, and then the man came out, placed the saddle on the horse and rode away.

Charlie waited, still as a cactus in the brush. The man, in a short ride, came back into sight, looked over everything, and made off again, apparently satisfied that there was no problem at hand.

Charlie waited one hour, made his way down to the cabin, slipped inside, and called Jordan's name. The rustling came from under the floor. He pulled up a few loose boards and saw Jordan bound and gagged in a hole in the ground, a sort of miner's lock-away he had seen before.

"Charlie, I knew you'd find my beads," Jordan said. "I knew

it. The man that grabbed me's gone to see a friend someplace. There was another man here sometime yesterday. They talked a long time. He's gone to meet him again."

Charlie said, "Go back that way. In the trees is another horse. Go home and tell your father where I am. I will watch for the man. I will leave a trail of this ..." and he held out a long yellow ribbon. I will leave many pieces of this. Show piece to your father. He will want this man. I will stay with him until your father find us. It is right your father catch man who steal son. Tell him now is time to bring army of men."

Jordan was three hours gone when the kidnapper came back, entered the cabin, started a fire, started to cook and, as Charlie might imagine the sight, pulled back the boards in the floor to see the hole empty, the boy gone.

The man rushed outside, looked around, and saw nothing, the Apache well hidden from his sight. The kidnapper desperately looked for signs in the ground, and found none. Charlie-Two-Horse had erased all the signs.

The man, in further haste, grabbed what gear he had, re-saddled his horse again and took off in a northerly direction. It was not the direction he had gone before.

Charlie-Two-Horse, reader of all signs, marker of trails, laid out the route of the man. Now and then, at a great distance, he caught sight of him cresting a hill, disappearing into a wadi, entering a canyon, or crossing a stream.

There was no way the kidnapper could lose the Apache who was following him.

After a night in the foothills of a mountain range, a small fire heating coffee, Charlie sat on a far place and kept watch. Two days later, in Timberville, in a saloon not far from the sawmill in full swing, Jesse Randolph Phillips and a small army of JRP ranch hands, along with a sheriff and two deputies, slipped into the Sawmill Saloon in a casual fashion, some loudly exclaiming they were glad the damned drive was over and it was time to wet their throats.

There was a lot of noise, a lot of shouting, and on the floor leading up to the bar, a minimal trail of pieces of tattered yellow ribbon ended at the backside of a man leaning over the bar, talking to the bartender.

He was heard to say, "I don't know where the hell he went,

Buck, but he disappeared and I wasn't going to hang around there."

A hand closed on his holster, another hand closed on his wrist, and a third had spun him around as Jess Randolph Phillips and his son Jordan Phillips walked in the door following a trail of yellow ribbon reduced to tatters.

Charlie-Two-Horse, first to get to the saloon, was sitting in one corner of the room, smiling at the boy who was more Apache than any other person in the room. And he wondered, as he fingered the beads collected in his pouch, if Jordan could string them together again to do more good prayer work.

Caleb Bonner, Loaner

Jed Horning, at the gate to his ranch in East Texas, eyed the lone rider heading his way across the grass from the direction of Pottsville. He'd been watching the rider for almost an hour coming along slowly as though he was smelling all the flowers, counting all the prairie dogs. Horning figured any man riding so slow brought an odd baggage with him, other than contemplation on horseback. Chances were it wasn't good news, with all that had been going on in the region for almost six months or more. Rustling had been rampant for a time, with murder along with it. Raising and selling cattle was his business, and trouble, of course, joined up sooner or later for the steady ride.

He wondered if the lone rider might even be a new chapter in an old business.

Horning, thick across the brow and the shoulder line, hair as gray as drifting clouds on ordinary days, did not recognize the approaching rider whose name was Caleb Bonner. Bonner was young and virile, handsome as a chieftain of a Plains tribe, quick as they come with his guns, eyes hazel green and alert as could be. Also, he came highly regarded in the hiring business, working for Mark Daniels, a big man with a big spread and a large ready force of cowpokes on a huge spread practically surrounding the town of Pottsville, 20 miles up-range. Bonner was his only "loaner," a man who could be hired, at a significant price, for a cause or a promise, or for a job that sometimes might include guarding and sometimes might include killing.

Bonner was the best "loaner" Daniels ever employed, coming out of Oklahoma half a dozen years earlier, the law on his trail, until that trail disappeared on Daniels' land. The law never knew what every Daniels' man knew; the fugitive was hidden in one of the two wells near the Daniels' ranch house until the law had departed. At that point he came up soaking wet but free and, henceforth, supposedly, swearing allegiance to Daniels.

Now, on another day, near noon, with little knowledge or foresight, Horning wondered what was coming at him, hoping it was not a bad situation just developing. His wife Dorothy and daughter Velma were back in the ranch house baking pies and cakes for a birthday party for Velma, 21 years old tomorrow, and as beautiful as

96

her mother 25 years earlier.

Horning shucked pesky thoughts and hailed the lone rider. "Hello, stranger. I'm Jed Horning and this is my spread. Anything I can do for you?" A quick idea framed itself in his mind that said nothing would surprise him. At the same time he noticed the clean cut about the young man, his shirt freshly laundered, hair trimmed, and shaved within a day or so. Not an ordinary cowpoke. Not a saddle tramp.

"Yes, sir. My name's Caleb Bonner and I work for Mark Daniels up around the Pottsville area. I was aiming to seek you out and say why I've come."

"That'd be right interesting for me to know," Horning said. "Want to come back to the house and have a coffee and a sandwich? My wife and daughter are heavy at cooking right now."

"Be my pleasure, Mr. Horning."

They rode the short ways jawing about weather, cattle by breed, any known acquaintances. Little came to light.

But when Velma Horning and Caleb Bonner made eye contact, Velma's mother, Dorothy Horning, understood only too well what had passed between two young people meeting for the first time.

She remembered when she first met Jed Horning … like it was yesterday, fresh as it ever was. Motherly instinct crowded her, wondering at that moment if her daughter was as lucky as she had been at the same kind of eye-opening meeting. A quick prayer rose up in her mind, even as she wondered who the young man really was. She remembered what her mother had said to her when she moved into her teens, about life in general and boys in particular: "Don't puddle jump." She never said it again.

In a few minutes of small talk, the four of them were comfortable, enjoying some sweets from the table, when Horning, holding up his hands, said, "So what brings you this way, son? You mentioned something on the ride in."

"Well, sir, Mr. Daniels took me aside and said he believes someone out this way is stealing his cattle. He wants to know if you have any ideas on it."

He dropped his eyes and raised them, and continued, "Not that he's accusing you," he quickly added defensively, his eyes caught up again by Velma, "but maybe somebody on your payroll is making a

97

few dollars on the side."

He moved his eyes in another gesture of defense, and qualified his words, "Or perhaps a neighbor's hired hands might be passing through your land with some stolen cows. I have to tell you that I saw a fence break on my way in here. Over by the wadi where three trees give good shade."

Velma Horning, across the table from Bonner and lit up like the morning sunset, jumped right in to protect the family and defend her father and his hired hands. "Not on your life," she said, her beautiful face suddenly set with an interior resolve. "I don't think a single man we've hired would rustle cattle from a neighbor or from anybody. Most of them have been here for a few years at least. They're all trustworthy. All good men."

Her tone changed immediately, as she carried on. "And how long have you been working 'on' the Daniels spread?" Her sarcasm was like a whip that lashed across the table. Her mother sat back, her father sat open-mouthed. The air nearly bubbled with feeling. It was as if she had said, "You work there, so why should you be here?"

Her blue eyes leveled at Bonner, who stared right back, a slight smile breaking at the corner of his mouth. He tried to find all the feelings that poured through him. "Six years, Miss. Six years. I do all kinds of things but never rustle cattle. Cattle make this end of the country turn green in more ways than one."

His smile became brighter and Dorothy Horning understood that singular brightness; admiration hung in its shine as the young man must have found Velma Horning to be an outspoken young lady with a mind of her own, a very special young lady, and lovely.

But something else, in front of her parents too, was happening to young Bonner. An entirely new something.

The lady knew it first; it was a gift long known to her, as it was known to mothers, to prime ladies of the land of known cultures and thus, in the wild west, hardly ever spoken of.

At a table in a Texas ranch house, something had changed, or at least had started a change amongst odd company.

In his few years, Caleb Bonner had been there for the action, right in the mix, in the thick of it; stared into the eyes of a puma ready to leap at him from close range overhead on a mountain trail, stared into the maddening eyes of a drunken gunman who held two pistols on him from the other side of a jail cell; sat directly in the

98

eyes of rampaging wild bulls and so many rambunctious horses he could not recount them. He'd been threatened with bullet and bow and arrow, rock slings, ax heads thrown with abandon, lead from unknown sources.

Though he was still unmarked.

Those impressions were indelible, dark and indelible, but the eyes of Velma Horning, from someplace near Heaven or Utopia, slid subtlely into him like none of the others. Did his face show it, he wondered? Were his cheeks red? Did his eyes show the heated reflections? Was his mission over before it had really started?

"Would you kill a rustler?"

"If he drew down on me."

"Is it worth it, a man for a cow? What if you're wrong about what he's going to do?"

"I'd rather be stupid alive than smart dead. What if they were to run off with all your father's cattle?"

"That's different."

"Because of the cost, the loss of cows you're planning to sell?"

Horning finally caught the eye of his wife, and vaguely understood what she was hinting at. He raised his hand again and said, "Do you have wire cutters in your saddle gear, son?"

"Of course I do. Every good cowpoke carries wire cutters for the job or for accidents if a cow gets caught up in the wire. Or a horse. Or another cowpoke. Why do you ask?"

"I was out there early this morning, son, and there was no cut wire anywhere along that fence. So it must have been done after I left and before you got there, or when you were there. Now I don't know when that could be except for close to the time you came through. That sound reasonable to you?"

"Sure does, Mr. Horning. And I didn't cut any wire any place today, on your land or elsewhere. And that's the honest truth."

Velma cut in to the discussion. "If somebody else saw you coming, Caleb, from way off, they could have cut the wire and try to blame it on you."

Dorothy Horning said, "So what should be done now?"

Bonner, without taking a breath, said, in an insistent voice, "Me and you, Mr. Horning, and some of your hands, ought to do some scatter walking over all that territory and see what's going on.

Somebody cut the wire for a reason. It wasn't me. It wasn't you, so let's see who it was."

The two men left the room, with Velma's eyes locked on Bonner and Dorothy Horning staring at her husband's back as he left the house. Their thoughts were on each man, hoping there'd be no trouble.

Horning and four of his hands, and Bonner, saddled up and left the barn, Horning saying as they rode, "We'll spread out to cover all the way to the river and off to the hills. A single shot means you're in trouble and you need help. Two shots quick together say you got somebody on the run, with cows or just plain suspicious. You all know who belongs and who don't."

He turned to Bonner and advised, "You stay with me because you don't know my other men. I got a fence rider out there, one gent in a line shack due for his relief and two brothers due back today from their sister's wedding over in Kilmartin Town. They might all be coming cross-range. I don't want any crazy killing going on. This whole thing sounds strange to me, but strange has been here before."

The men spread out and Horning looked at Bonner. "How many men you killed, son?"

"Three," Bonner said. "They were slower than me and meaner than me and the odds didn't favor them, though I told each one of them all of that."

"They didn't listen?"

"They never do, not when there's more than one of them and only one of you."

They had been apart from the other men for less than half an hour, when a single shot rang out, coming their way from the edge of the foothills, off to the north.

Horning, straight up in the saddle, said, "Let's go this way," and he pointed right at the origin of the gunshot." He started to go in that direction when Bonner said, "Not directly at the sound, Mr. Horning, Let's edge up this way, toward that cluster of trees and come in from that end. It's probably safer that way, and if there's real trouble there, we don't want to walk right into it."

Horning was going to say something he immediately thought he might regret. Instead he said, "Okay, we'll do it your way."

In a matter of minutes they had a view of one of Horning's men protecting himself behind a rock with three men trying to edge
100

in on him without firing their weapons. In the opening of a wadi dipping into a low area were perhaps two dozen head of cattle.

Bonner, in a low whisper, said, "They want to get your man without firing any shots if they can. They don't want to scatter the cattle."

At that moment Bonner saw two of Horning's men approaching and waved them down, pointing ahead of them. Horning seconded the wave and the men dismounted, tied their horses off, and began approaching a large stone outcropping, looking like a good place to defend themselves, or check out the signaled trouble.

After tying off their horses, Bonner took his rifle from the saddle scarab and he and Horning moved slowly toward the strangers. Bonner, leading the way, had his rifle at his shoulder, ready to get off an accurate as well as an instant shot if necessary. More than once he motioned Horning behind him, until they were behind two good sized trees, the strange men clearly in sight, no more than 30 or 40 yards away.

Bonner, calm as anyone could ever be, pursed his lips to hold Horning in silence, and stepped out into plain sight with the rifle at his shoulder.

One of the strangers, sensing more than seeing him, started to turn around and Bonner put a round right between his legs, pumped a second shot at the man next to him, and yelled out, "The next one catches one of you in the chest, I'm not saying which one, and high up where it will hurt like hell. Now drop your weapons. There are half a dozen of us out here around you and we don't want you dying before the trial."

He put a third round right between the legs of the third man.

They dropped their guns, and saw Horning's two men coming from their positions. A third rider of Horning's rode right into the situation with guns drawn.

Hands down, it was hands up for the strangers.

At the table that evening, Bonner invited and dinner over, Horning told the story at least a dozen times, all with variations of one sort or another, but all with the step-up and step-in details about Bonner.

Dorothy Horning, in a glorious mood, kept her eyes on her daughter and the dashing young man, still aware of questions hanging about him and his past. The motherly instinct kept working

101

on her, even with her high regard for Caleb Bonner this newest incident had stimulated. She had to bring them all out, dig into all of it for her daughter's sake.

Her voice carried deep concern, when she said, "You told Velma you had some kind of a problem back there in Oklahoma. Something to do with the law. What was that all about, Mr. Bonner?"

Dorothy Horning, at that moment in her life, was indeed the matriarch of her realm, her dinner table, her dining room, her home, her daughter who leaned on the verge of newness, excitement, a quick change in her own life.

Even then, Bonner felt warm in her company; she was a most attractive woman, like her daughter, and not yet rounded but still fairly slim … which boded well for Velma. Each one of the women's eyes were totally attentive, their sweet lips were enticing even sitting demurely pursed. His comfort zone, he realized, was growing. If his observations escaped either woman outwardly, they were most likely aware of them on some level that women shared.

Bonner looked her right in the eye and answered, "It was a big mistake that some scoundrel dropped at my feet. Mr. Daniels kept me from getting caught by a wild posse and found out the truth about what went on back in Oklahoma. Even a sheriff was in on it because it was a relative of his that messed things up for me. That's all squared away. I've paid my debt to Mr. Daniels. I've told him so a few times and he understands. I'm not wanted anyplace for any crime, but if a man draws down on me, he better be ready. That's just how I feel about things."

Mother and daughter were smiling at each other in a way that Horning did not catch.

Instead, in a sudden grasp at reality on a different approach, said, "Caleb, do you think the men we caught today were the ones that your boss sent you after? They haven't let on a thing other than they found a cut wire and found some cattle in one of the low spots and that was outside the fence. They say they didn't rustle any cattle and the signs point to that. Neither your or me saw any cattle tracks near that break, so it throws me for a loss. Can you add anything to that?"

"No, I can't. Not now. Maybe they really aren't the real bad guys, but they had guns drawn. Maybe it was self-defense on their part too. We reacted to the whole scene out in front of us. It might

102

take a good man to find all that out." He held off on the balance of his statement, stressing a point to his listeners, and then finally said, "Not everybody is a bad guy."

Horning said, "Do you know anybody that could do that for me? Perhaps a man to be hired for the job." An enlightening smile had crossed his face as if he was the first person to have such an idea.

Velma Horning simply said, "I do and I'm looking right at him," as her mother folded up all her curiosity issues and put them neatly away, like her dinner napkins would go back into their little box on the top of the buffet.

Clay Hartung, Kid Wrangler

Clay Hartung's father said, on many occasions when talk turned to the family around a campfire or at a saloon with pals, "The boy was born on a horse, as far as I know. I was away on a drive at the time and his mother never told me anything different." He'd chuckle and always add his final word, "The lady knew her way around the horses, too. You can say he was born with saddle and reins in his blood."

When he was 16 by a few days he was chosen wrangler for Austin Peary's second drive up the Chisholm Trail from his ranch near San Antonio, Texas to Abilene, Kansas, the railhead of the Kansas Pacific Railway. Hartung, as noticed by Peary on his first drive, was a master horseman from every angle, in the saddle, with the reins and with a rope. A few of the boys said he talked to horses in their language, as if the sensation of a hand gesture or a simple cough or shrug was enough of a message to be obeyed. "That boy's got somethin' goin' on with all them horses, you ask me," one of the older hands declared.

"You know what I expect of you, son?" Peary spoke directly on the day of the hire, without any curves in his talk, and wanted answers the same way.

"Yes, sir, I do," Hartung said in reply. "Tend the horses so drovers never lack one. When danger comes, make sure I keep as many as possible in my control, where I can see and protect them."

"You do that, son, and I'll see that your share is counted out clean and accurate. You do your job and I'll do mine."

They shook hands.

At the end of the drive Peary's cattle would be sold and shipped eastward from that railhead at Abilene. Hartung had about 80 horses to take care of in Peary's remuda, each one had to be available as quickly as possible for a rider switching mounts or needing a new mount. Thus, the horses had to be kept separate from the cattle, each drover needing about 5 or 6 horses set aside for him for the duration of the drive.

Even before the drive started, Hartung had to train horses to accept his commands, like allowing flimsy restrictions to contain them, such as a simple rope enclosure or long tethers. Out on the grass, Hartung had to keep the remuda confined in some manner, usually by a hasty rope fence on good grass, which also had a hand in holding hungry animals in place.

As wrangler he had to know the horses each drover favored and be able to recognize them immediately at exchange, which could come up any time. Thus, he had to be good with a rope to catch and hold a horse, be able to saddle up quickly while the drover might visit the chow wagon. Now and then he could lean on the ramrod for help, usually an older man who was capable of every task on a drive, drover to cook, scout to doctor, ride drag or take the lead. But a wrangler was responsible at all times for the horses on a drive.

Out on the trail 16 days later, the first interruption came from a small group of Indians looking for meat on the hoof. They took three head with them in their flight, Peary nodding his head as if the exchange was acceptable. But the attempt at getting some of the horses did not go well with them, as Hartung managed to get all his remuda tucked safely into a small canyon when the Indians first made their intentions known, rising up from the depths of a wadi without having been seen by the lead scout, who had missed their signs and passed them by.

That did not set well with Peary. He chewed out the lead man for at least a half hour and finished by saying, "You get one more chance, Henry, and then you get drag if you don't work it out. You could be there until we have to carry you home."

Henry ate alone, away from the fire, then mounted up slowly and went out to do his share of night riding. Hartung, watching him disappear into the shadows of evening, checked his rope enclosure for the third time. He'd check again and again before night was over.

The next six days went fairly smooth, with a regular march each day, Peary apparently pleased with the distance traveled daily. He was talkative at the campfire, every so often halting his talk to listen to a soft lullaby coming from the edge of the herd, a night rider singing an old favorite, the cattle still, the stars wide awake in the velvet sky.

"Ain't that some kind of a song, boys?" he said. "Makes me think of a neighbor when I was a kid back home, sitting alone on his dark porch and putting the whole night to sleep and everything in it."

"Did you hear those songs all the way through, Boss?"

Peary thought about that and said, "Some of those songs are the kind you never hear the end of, they do the job so good."

He rolled over on his blanket and fell asleep, the lullaby out on the grass fading away in the darkness, the stars in their slow roll across the heavens, the cattle still and silent.

The idyllic scene was broken up hours later with gunshots and the thundering sound of cattle rushing ahead of the gunshots, and a lot of yelling and men rushing into boots and calling for their horse and Clay Hartung up and in the saddle and holding his horses in the rope enclosure. Drovers mounted in a hurry, headed out to head off the stampeding cattle.

Six rustlers were trying to drive much of the herd onto wide open grass, one column of cattle breaking for the north and another heading almost due south, the herd split as planned.

Peary motioned to three men and they headed south along one part of the stampede, firing guns at intervals, trying to turn the herd back. Other men headed after the northward herd, all of them aware of the split-up attempt of the rustlers to divide not only the herd, but the company of drovers, and the remuda as well.

Hartung sat his horse, waiting for the attempt to run off his horses onto the prairie. In a piece of skyline light of the false dawn, he saw a rider coming down an incline near his horses. He rode straight at the last point where he had seen the other rider, and pulled his rifle from the scabbard. He held his horse beside one huge rock and as the mystery rider came by him, he knocked him out of the saddle with one swing of his rifle, butt first.

He had protected the remuda without firing a shot. "So far, so good," he said to himself, thinking about the situation as he headed back to the temporary enclosure, hoping the rustlers had assigned just the one man to get the remuda on the run.

He found the horses excited, straining at their ropes, but holding in place. His presence seemed to calm them as the sound of gunshots, flatter, duller, came from further away, out on the wide prairie.

It took a few hours of hard work, some daring and clever riding, and accurate firing of weapons, but the rustlers were driven off, the herd re-gathered, and morning came with high sunshine.

When Peary and some of the drovers came back to camp, the chuck wagon busy, they found 16-year old Clay Hartung, drive wrangler, keeping company with a trussed up and hurting stranger sitting beside the fire. The stranger looked to be in considerable pain, remnants of blood on his face as well as on his shirt.

"He tried for the horses, Boss, but he didn't get far," Hartung said. "I didn't ask him any questions. Figured I'd leave that to you."

Peary nodded, looked at his trail boss and said, "What do you figure, Smiley?"

"A hundred head loose somewhere, but not with that gang. We run them clean out of here. Won't be long I get most of them back. Leave a few for the Cherokee, Choctaw, or maybe Chickasaw. I saw them sitting up there." Smiley Wescott nodded to the foothills. "I'd guess them to be Cherokee, but I ain't sure."

"That's good hoping and good thinking, Smiley. Take who you want with you."

Wescott sidle up to Peary and said, "The kid did a hell of a job, Boss, knocking our guest right out of the saddle without firing a shot. When you talk to our sore company here, ask him who was in the gang. See if you can find out if Bart Tuskin was one of them. I thought I recognized an old saddle pard. I see him again, I'll run him in as a rustler. He never was too honest to begin with. This one's name is Scotty O'Donnell. I got that much out of him."

Wescott signaled to two men and the trio rode off.

Peary, standing above the captured rustler O'Donnell and said, "I'm not going to spend too much of my time with you, son. I got cows to move, but if I was you I'd tell me in a hurry who was with you. You know they ain't coming back for you. So you best tell me who was with you, or I turn you over to the kid again. I know he won't be so careful next time. I just told him to bring me a prisoner and he plain old-fashioned got me one. Tell me who was with you. If one of them's Bart Tuskin, you won't have to tell me. But I'll make sure they figure you did. He one of them?"

"Yeh, he was with us. Purly Yates set it up."

"Where'll they hole up?"

"Up in the Mescalili country, in a cabin in one of them canyons. Miners were there once."

"Well, son," Peary said, "I'm not letting you go now, and I don't like the idea of feeding you and having a man watch you all the time, unless it's the kid. But when we get this herd delivered, we're going up after them owl hoots. I'll let you go then, but of course the gang will know you told us. We'll make sure of that, so when the time comes, you better make fast tracks out of this country or they'll

107

be after you like their own posse."

When the cattle were delivered to Abilene, Peary told his men what he was about to do concerning the rustlers. They all agreed to a man that something had to be done. As they were about to go off on the hunt, Hartung approached Peary and said, "Boss, can I talk to for a few minutes, away from the others." The two rode off to the shade of a tree and talked for 15 minutes.

"Are you sure about this, Clay? Think this is the way to go."

"I do, Boss. It's a cinch."

Three days later, shy of Mescalili country, Hartung began to race his horse back and forth across the prairie. Finally, after an arduous ride, he rode off in an easterly direction, his horse heated, tired from the run. About an hour later, after another shorter run, he rode his horse into the Mescalili canyon where the hide-out was located.

A look-out spotted him easily and warned the others. They surrounded Hartung quickly and brought him to a cabin at the deep end of the canyon.

"Who are you kid? What are you doing here?" one man said, obviously the leader of the pack.

"Hell," said Hartung, "I found a couple of longhorns and was selling them to a farmer, a squatter, and he pointed out the brand on them. I never noticed them before. He sent his son to get the sheriff, so I split out of there in a hurry. I hope no one followed me."

"Why'd you come up here? What was that brand the squatter saw? I got lots of questions for you, kid."

"The brand was AP Square. I never saw it before. I ain't never been up this side of the country. I just wanted to get out of the way if I could. This looked like a good place."

"What's your name, kid?"

"Clay Brady. From nowhere in general. Been alone for years, since my old man ran out on me."

"Well, kid, my old man did the same thing. My name's Purly Yates. This here's Paulie and that's Butch and this ugly one over here is Bart Tuskin. We're interested in that herd or what's left of it."

"Well, there's more than a hundred of them in a canyon back down the trail. I was able to drive them into the back end of the canyon and fence them up with some blow downs. But there's no way I could handle them all, so I figured I could do a few at a time. I guess I picked on an honest squatter, not that you can find that many out this way."

"You're okay, kid," Yates said. "We can join up and get them cattle into the right hands. We'll share the cut. Be a piece of cake, them drovers long gone on their way."

Hartung smiled and said, "Sounds great to me. Maybe I can get to talk to that squatter again, if you don't mind."

"You're okay, kid. Sure, give him a piece of your mind. Ha, that's good. Serve him right for blabbing."

It was in the early evening, with enough tracks showing traffic on the way into the selected canyon, that the rustlers were pinned down by a solid crossfire and threw their guns down.

Hartung, leading the gang toward the blow downs at the end of the canyon, was able to duck in behind a sheaf of rock and hide from the cross fire.

Trussed and tossed on their saddles and on the way to justice, the rustlers were quiet until Yates said, "That kid lead us into this?"

"No, he really didn't," Peary offered. "It was one of your own that did that, Scotty O'Donnell, the one you sent after his horses. He got knocked clean out of the saddle by the kid, who's my wrangler right now. Next drive, next year, he's apt to be my trail boss. Boy's got a lot going for him besides horses."

"Oh. Yeah," Purly Yates said. "How old is he?"

Peary qualified his answer, saying, "His pa says he's 16. Could be 60 on a good day for all I know. But today's one of his good days. You got to agree with me on that."

His horse went down at last; the great, friendly and courageous beast with his last breath had taken him into the canyon and dropped dead. "You even saved me a bullet, Red," Burt Clanwood said, as he piled what loose rocks he could find atop the corpse of Red Herman, his mount for almost 7 of his 25 years, in the hole he had died in.

A tear in his eye found a small place in his cheek to start a roll. One tear. "Not a lot, Red, but I'm not a crying man. You know that, horse. You know that."

He patted the last stone in place, a round, weighty stone that might hold off the scavengers for a few days. Or, he thought, until the sun got to it and the heat and the stink drew all kinds of carrion hunters, from spiders and ants right up to the high flyers. He looked overhead to see if any of the big wings had spotted Red Henry's site yet.

Clanwood, standing tall after his task, almost 6 feet, good looking and tanned a decent light brown on his face and arms, turned his back and walked deeper into the canyon. A wide Stetson sat on his head, a gray shirt and a black vest on his torso, heavy-looking pants below, and spurs on tall boots. He had his rifle, his saddlebag, his sidearm, but the saddle was still on his horse. There was no way he could have gotten it out of the hole with the posse somewhere near. He had no idea where he was or what was going on in the turmoil that was his life also on the trail behind him.

He figured he didn't know much at the time.

Except, he knew this was Wyoming, or Idaho. Except he knew it was July, or pretty close. Except there was at least a remnant of a posse on his trail. Except he had nothing to show him the way to someplace else. Except he was thirsty and hungry and could sleep for two weeks or two months.

The strange, funny, totally ridiculous part of the whole thing was he had committed no crime. His spit hadn't even missed the spittoon in the last saloon he'd been in. He was clean of crime, and even the thought of it.

In the innards of a small crevice, at least six feet up off the ground, he had managed to lie down. Squeezing up and squeezing in, drawing a knee and an elbow as tight and as close to his body as he

110

could, he squeezed up and in. The metal of his spurs made tinkling sounds, scraping sounds, lively sounds. Breathing was possible, pleasurable. He sucked on one finger until he thought he had generated enough saliva to wet his throat. He thought of the spittoon again. He thought of spitting again. One leg was burning with an unseen fire. Maybe the spot where a bullet had nicked him, maybe a muscle was just plain sore. Hell, he was sore all over. How would he ever sleep?

He didn't even count himself alive. No visions. No images. Not a single face to disturb any sleep. He just slept. He did not say his name. Made no pleas. Said no jokes. Counted his breaths until they were no longer countable. Slept.

Burt Clanwood slept. Without Red Henry as much a watchdog as any mutt, he slept.

It could have been hours, days, minutes.

At length, something called attention, came intelligible.

The slight, scratching sound woke him. He smelt something that was alive. Not cooked, but could be.

The sound came again. From below him. From Red Henry's last place on earth.

The rifle sat behind him, pointed the wrong way. Straining one arm, drawing it along his waist, he touched the butt of his pistol in its holster, a holster he had managed to slide onto his waist as he had crept to this tight chamber. The pistol came away in his hand, a delicate, balanced, sense of weight that teased him. He hoped he had a round in the chamber. One round.

With one eye he spotted a snake at Red Henry's site; a rattler whose body gleamed in the setting; bright sunlight lingered on the creature. He saw brown and red and green markings.

With aggravated silence and pain, he aimed the pistol, squeezed the trigger, and killed the snake. The gunshot echoed in the rocks like a base drum was beating in his ears.

Soon he would eat.

The fire started easily from dry tinder and brush, flared up quickly, and the rattler, after high heat was reached, went into a sizzle that also sounded in the canyon like a small echo. The aroma rose with the sound too, a not unpleasant smell he had known before a number of times. Once it had been with Charlie Two Swords at the edge of the Tetons. He had no idea how far away The Tetons were,

111

and could only guess northerly, direct northerly from where he chewed on his meal. Charlie Two Swords said a rattler had to be cut in small chunks and cooked for a long time. "Don't rush the snake, ever, and he won't rush you," Charlie had said, and he smiled when he said those words, hoping his intention was understood.

The meat was chewy but tasty with a sprinkle of salt from his saddle bag. It was all he had along with a small pouch of coffee.

Thinking of coffee had a problem attached to it. His canteen was under Red Henry, most likely crushed with the added weight of the piled rocks. He again argued with himself that they'd been no time to grasp any more than his rifle and saddle bag.

With a bit of gusto he finished off most of his meal, before he realized the cooking odor had obviously climbed the walls of the canyon, and was going where any breath of air might take it.

That's when Clanwood heard a thin, distant sound coming from somewhere inside the canyon. Quickly he set the remnants of the snake meal on a flat rock, grabbed his rifle and saddlebag and crept back up into the fissure where he had spent the night. Hiding was preferable to a face-off or stand-up fight, if those were the options.

Decision time told him that waiting out was preferable to scouting around. He'd lay low and wait for developments; the snake had come to him, so maybe coffee would, in some fashion or another. It made for a pleasant but long wait. The sun passed overhead and disappeared as an object behind a rock wall.

It was the mad singing that made its way to him, somewhat boisterous, not really tuneful, but human music. He did not know how far away it was coming, from what area of the canyon or the walls of the canyon, there were so many hollows such as the one in which he had made his bed for one night.

And it was not one voice he heard. It was harmony; two voices singing in the bowels of the canyon, uproarious happy voices. The words, at first, were unintelligible, but they rounded themselves into shape in quick order. He pictured the voices coming around the corner of some huge rock or a wall of stone sheared off the face of the canyon thousands of years ago and found itself planted just for this duet, this duo, not drunk, but hilariously happy in their singing.

Then their conversational talk sounded in the canyon, the first spoken words he had heard in days.

112

"Hey, Willie," one of the voices said, thick, guttural, mountain-like, "you smell what I smell? Someone's been cookin' snake and left some for us. Lookie here. A rattler, or what's left o' him, rolled and burnt good enough for tastin'. Whatdya think of that, Willie? Whatdya think of that?"

Clanwood expected to hear hands clapping, a back being slapped vivaciously.

"Well, Mort," a second voice replied, "he's got to be hidin' from us, right here in these here rocky places. Couldn't get too far from here, could he you think?"

Clanwood, intrigued now, thankful for hearing friendly talk from friendly folk, inched himself forward in the tight crevice. He was above the two men and had a good look at them, the singing duet. He almost laughed at the thought. Their age was a mystery to him, them being so well-bearded. They could be in their late forties or their early sixties, he thought. Their stances and erect postures gave him no clue except that they were not too old for life in the mountains. But, above all, they weren't posse, but were mountain men who did not much like town life, except for an occasional supply run and a wetting down.

"If he ain't disappeared himself an' still hangin' around here, I hope he got some coffee, but I ain't smelled any yet."

Clanwood, able to satisfy someone's wish, and knowing for a fact they weren't posse, yelled out from his high hiding place, "Wait there, gents. I'll be right down, and I got some coffee in my kit. Long as you ain't part of that posse that's been chasing me for something I didn't do."

There was a flurry of excitement down below Clanwood, "You hear that, Mort, some strange dude's got coffee, real coffee, 'n' more than that burnt-wood coffee you been throwin' my way." He paused and said, "Mort, we're havin' a party with real coffee. We got jerky and sourdough biscuit for soft'ning." He threw his head back and said to the heavens, "Well, what else has this day brung us?"

Getting free from cramped quarters, dragging and hauling his gear with him, Clanwood managed to scramble down to meet the two mountain men. They were a rugged, bearded pair looking to be strong as a pair of oxen, with blue eyes on both like night stars in a dark sky. Fur caps sat on their heads and they wore a lot of fur about their torsos and on the legs. One of them wore store boots and the other wore thick moccasins of a dark brown color.

Their tongues were hanging out.

"I'm Burt Clanwood running ahead of a posse for something I didn't do. My horse ran himself to death and just fell down in a hole back there and I had to pile up some rock to keep him from critters of all kinds. My canteen was under him and I couldn't make coffee but I sure will be glad to get some in me now. You got water?"

"Sure do, son," one said. "I'm Mort Bonney and this ugly dude's my pard. His name is Willie Plaistow."

Clanwood laughed and said to Willie Plaistow, "I heard you say that your friend here has been making burnt-wood coffee for you. What's that?"

"Well, son, it sure ain't burnt and it sure ain't wood and it sure ain't coffee, but long's we got meat or biscuits for soft'ning, it's tolerable for a while." With a quizzical look still on Clanwood's face, he added, "Mort has some favorite growth he soaks in tarn water and dries in the sun with some other stuff he's handy with and crushes it to make a kind of dust when it's dried up and calls it burnt-wood coffee.

Bonney said, "What sheriff is pushing after you, Burt? Is it Charlie Max?"

"That's him," said a surprised Clanwood. "You know him?"

"Know enough about him to know he ain't comin' up in here to Dead Canyon. Charlie Two Swords told him way back he was goin' to get hisself kilt up here chasin' the wrong customer if he knowed it was the wrong customer an' him often runnin' off at the mouth about who could be guilty, an' not always who would be guilty."

"You know Charlie Two Swords?" The further surprise was in Clanwood's voice as he loosened a rawhide string on a pouch of coffee and the aroma filled the air as if it had swept in on the wind.

"Hell, son," Bonney said, "anybody up in these mountains knows Charlie Two Swords. Where'd you meet him? He ever doctor you? That man can fix everythin' 'ceptin' broken hearts an' broken toes." His eyes lit up. "Smell that coffee, Willie. The party's gonna start." He did a quick little jig with his booted feet.

Plaistow piled some more wood on the fire and whipped a coffee pot that most likely had been through several skirmishes and

114

several wars. He filled it with water from a canteen and measured out seven caps of coffee from Clanwood's coffee bag and poured each one into the coffee pot like he was in the kitchen. When the pot was settled in place, he tied the thong on the coffee bag, looked at Clanwood imploringly, and smiled when Clanwood nodded. He stuck the bag inside his fur wrap of sorts, like a gold deposit had been made.

The coffee aroma heightened its delicious grasp on the men, and they shared a few quiet moments sharing the brew. Hard biscuits softened in the second cup, and dried meat, heated on the fire, made up the balance of their meal. Moments of silence hung about the three men.

Clanwood, his hunger and thirst about bated, finally said, "Tell me more about Charlie Two Swords. Why is he like he is, doing what he does, like he works on both sides of the wire."

"Charlie knows times are achangin' an' does his best to treat any man the way he likes himself treated. He ain't no uppity injun lookin' for a way out. More like a way in, if you get my drift on it. Says his god up there on the mountain top is the same god for any man whether he looks up there or not."

"What tribe's he from?"

Plaistow replied, "He ain't never said. He's just plain good old Indian you can count on when times get itchy. We been there some, aye Mort?"

There were nods and another silence, as if things said needed to be soaked in, dwelt on, owned. And young Clanwood suddenly knew some new intelligence had entered his life. He said nothing until Bonney, after a long spell of looking off into the canyon, said, "We'll get your saddle out from under your horse. You'll need a saddle when we get you a horse."

"Where'll we get horses up in here?" Clanwood said, another surprise loose on him.

"We got a couple of ladies over in the next canyon keepin' mind on a few horses an' a couple of meat cows. They're good ladies an' never stole nothin' from us. But we'll need your saddle. We'll tend that soon's coffee's gone. We ain't got but two saddles."

"I'm not about to go down into one of those towns where Charlie Max hangs around."

"Don't worry none about him, son. We'll find out what's

115

happenin' with him. You stay up here with the ladies. We run out of coffee two days ago and it's near time we went to town, so we'll get a taste o' things down there."

In a few hours the three men had the saddle removed from Red Henry's body, the canteen indeed crushed, the carrion hunters already at work. They piled the rocks back on top of the horse, and went on their way, into the next canyon, where a grassy area ran wide until the walls narrowed, a fence of brush and split poles ran side to side, animals roamed inside, and two Indian maidens, as young as Clanwood, waved at them as they passed through a rough gate.

"Them ladies are our daughters, Burt. That's what keeps us friends. Their mothers was kilt by a renegade whose name ain't important no more an' we strung him on the face of the canyon for three days 'fore he died one miserable death he was owed. So be careful with their hearts. Like I said, Charlie Two Swords can fix most anythin' 'ceptin' broken toes and broken hearts. Tall one's name is Blue Leaf and the other is Dove Calling. They ain't never seen nothin' like you, son, so don't make no mistakes."

So they had a good meal that evening, with steak and potatoes and corn and another two pots of coffee, great coffee, and Burt Clanwood, the loner, began to fall in love. It came with nightfall, sly as a whisper, easy as a soft solution on the skin, an elixir as fine as any that one could imagine.

But the poor lad, new to love, didn't know which one it was, Blue Leaf or Dove Calling. The dilemma was thoroughly enjoyable for a young man so recently on the run, who had lost his grand horse, and who had squeezed himself into a rocky place in a dead canyon to sleep away one night.

He found himself looking with great favor on both maidens for the three days that their fathers, Bonney and Plaistow, were away being "citified for a small duration."

Both of the maidens were lovely, wholesomely lovely, with hair as black and as shiny as a night sky, slender the way prairie flowers sat in a soft breeze, sweet in the face as a whole hive of honey. But one began to wend her way into his heart. He tried to measure the whats and hows, but was unable to distinguish the differences at first. At length it proved to be unsaid words on the corner of one of their mouths, the way her hips moved with unsaid

116

words, how her hands, without words, could tell him a story he fully understood. He could feel the luck he never had come into his mind.

And the dread that such luck might propose in its acceptance.

Blue leaf was the first to notice the drama floating around her, and when their fathers came back from their "due visitation" she said, "Dove Calling has a husband in sight. I believe they love each other, but they may not know it yet."

Bonney nodded his understanding and said, "There's a doctor in town, a nice man, who needs the wisdom you have. We'll visit soon. An' we can tell young Burt the sheriff, Charlie Max, got shot an' killed by the man he should have been chasin'. That part of his life is over. I think he's gonna be a mountain man now."

His smile was wide and good and he said, "The new part can begin as soon as they want."

Brace Danby, Pony Rider

It was June of 1861, turmoil running across the land all the way from the big-citied East. Not far from Hayes Jackson's Bar-B-Bell ranch in a northern corner of Colorado, a rider on a galloping pinto came up out of wadi and headed down the worn trail leading to the town of Broken Eye. One of Jackson's cowpokes, 16-year old Brace Danby, saw the rider tottering in the saddle. From the same way came two other riders firing at the pinto rider. When Danby rode into their sight, the two men opened fire at him. He dropped off his horse with rifle in hand, an experienced hunter and marksman, and dropped one man right out of the saddle. When he hit the horse of the second man, the man leaped off the horse before it fell to the ground and ran into a wooden tract. The young cowpoke chased the supposed bandit with a shot at his feet before he disappeared.

Ahead of him Danby saw the pinto rider fall from the saddle. The fall was clumsy, disjointed, like a trick rider doing a strange maneuver. It carried different messages. Danby raced to him, assuring that the bandit afoot was out of sight. The fallen rider was a wiry, thin youngster no older than Danby. He was bleeding so much he was shaking, and his eyes had gone hollow with dread on his face, as if he had seen all this before he even got where he was.

Struggling to talk, a hand waving in support of that effort, he managed to say, "Pony rider. Get my package to Southby at Gilman Forks Station. It's got to get to California." He pointed where his horse had run off a ways. "It's in the mochila, the pouch on my saddle. It's important as all get-out."

With alarm on his face, and the most beseeching look he could muster, the fallen rider said, "Do it for me, fella. I'm sworn."

The wounded rider passed out.

Danby chased down the loose horse, roped the young rider on it and hurried back to the ranch. "Take care of him, Harry," he yelled to another hand, "he's one of them mail boys and I got to get to his next stop."

As he hopped on his own horse, with the mail pouch the boy had called a mochila, he yelled out, "There's a dead robber out on the trail I shot, and a dead horse and another robber on foot. Tell the boss to watch out for him. He don't have his horse anymore. I'll be back sometime. Them's the ones that shot this boy." He raced off. A new sensation, he knew, was burning inside him as he lit out for the Gilman Forks Pony Station.

For about a year Danby had seen lone riders of the Pony Express, as it had been called, sprinting past the Bar-B-Bell spread, stopping for nothing or nobody, often waving when they passed by him and some of the ranch cows he was moving or checking on. The sight, coming up just about every week, from what the ranch hands were saying, created a little excitement in Danby. He wondered what it would feel like to be entrusted with getting a pack of mail as far along the journey as he could in the shortest amount of time.

Now he'd find out.

The horse under him sped fast, bringing breeze and air flow straight onto his face. The rush exhilarated him every time he closed his eyes for a second, to keep dust and debris out of them. In those moments he brought back images of things moving fast that he had seen in his short life; cattle and bison, both in huge herds, rushing across the grass in a wave of panic or hurry, driven by some inner demand of escape or salvation, perhaps wolves, Indians, or rustlers at their work, and the sound beating into his ears like drums, the land itself vibrating with the roll of sound. Lines of troops came back he had also seen rushing to the rescue of people in distress, the waving blue of their uniforms like huge needles sewing up the countryside, bending and dipping and swinging wide at certain features of the landscape.

The awe in him about the whole situation ... the shooters, the deaths, the pony boy, the mochila, the messages, the destination ... came up in him as an unequalled exhilaration. It puffed him, making him lean lower, reducing the resistance coming upon him the way his father had shown him years ago, and which now freed this horse to sprint faster in a race against time.

The seconds ticked away. The minutes. The breath in his lungs. A tree he had marked. A dip in the trail. The point where he had last seen an Indian only six months ago.

In one huge gulp of air he realized the clump of cottonwoods, once ahead of him a long way on the trail, perhaps ten minutes away, maybe more, was suddenly behind him; the same thing happened to a huge rock rolled into the middle of the grass by some ungodly powerful force so far back in time he could not count back to it. It too was suddenly behind him, the horse doing its job, flying across

119

the grass, down a section of dusty trail, past a sheaf of rock where a ledge of stone had ruptured the ground in a huge thrust, only to settle back forever as an outcropping to mark the way. His way west. The pony boy's way west. If the pony boy had been this way before, had he seen this same piece of ledge? Marked it? Thought of it later on, how it stood out at the side of the trail?

Now and then he saw a skull decorating the landscape with its signal of time. A wagon, broken by time and weather, fallen in its journey, was now returning to earth, like a man might do if not tended at death. He wondered more than once how many graves he might have galloped over in his rides out upon the Earth itself. Once at a campfire, his father had said, "We move west on the graves of those who went before us. When you pass by a marker, think of the man or woman that had come to that place, with dreams unfulfilled … then count yourself lucky that your journey is still ahead of you."

At another release from the oncoming zephyrs, he caught hold again of a force of Indians coming down off a high rise in a flanking movement against a group of troops, saw them expert at riding. Their colors had gone awash on the plains, their feathers on parade, hawks and eagles in the wash of motion, crows filled with night, cardinal red, jay blue, owls owned by arrow or quiver. Their formations obeyed one order, their colors obviously stolen from rainbows coming after a rare rain, or even after a wind storm, beating them into hiding.

His mind filled.

Danby leaned into those remembered sights, those images, every one of them, felt their force and unity coming into one cause, felt the sense of power they must have known battling against an enemy.

The ride he was on soared above everything, made itself prime motivator and annunciator. If there was a fist, he was in it: the message, the mochila, the rider, the horse, the destination.

Now him, it was. Now him. Not the pony boy, but him. Brace Danby. Motherless. Fatherless. Brotherless. Sisterless. Alone on the trail.

It all leaped again. The force of it. The long ride. The horse whose heart might burst. The unknown scene ahead of him at arrival at Gilman Forks Station. How would he handle that? How would they handle him, new to it all?

At odd times he heard the pony boy's words coming back to him, saying again, "Hurry," and "I'm sworn." At such repeated sounds, Danby spurred the horse again, time standing in his face, time pushing him from behind, trying to catch up to him. Then came the pony boy's words like a Gattling gun cutting loose. "Hurry, I'm sworn." Again and again, "Hurry, I'm sworn." "Hurry, I'm sworn."

A sense of awe hit Danby as he wondered about the pony boy. It made him say aloud, into the teeth of the wind, "How does his mind keep him company on such long rides, such long hours? Does he have the thoughts I have? Or see the visions I see? What keeps him going? I hope he's all right, that the cook did his best for him with the little doctoring he's had."

His mind flew back to the Jackson ranch. Had he left a good thing too far behind? For what purpose? How would he justify his quick move to take over another man's job, another boy's job? How would the boss take it?

Over the top of a slow rise, as the horse labored nearing the end of his run, he saw the station ahead. A man stood out front, waving him on, the reins of a horse in his hands. The man waved again, drawing him on, spurring him, in fact.

Danby pulled the horse to a stop right where the man stood beside a small corral.

"You've fallen behind. You're late." His stare fell on Danby's face. "Ya new, ain't ya? I was looking for Kid Hoskins this trip. Where's he at? What's ya name?"

He didn't wait for an answer, but whipped the mochila off the horse and slapped it onto the horse whose reins he was holding. "Mount up," he said. They'll be waitin' ya. Here's a bag of grub for the fly and a full canteen. They be waiting at Mercy Creek Station, 'nother dozen miles or more. Straight as an arrow from here, between them two passes up there on both sides of ya. Good luck. They'll tell ya about the next leg."

He slapped the horse on the rump when Danby mounted. The new horse leaped ahead like a race starter had set him off, his head down, pulling the new weight slight as it was. The burst of energy from the new horse moved right into Danby's bloodstream. It pounded in him. With it, with this new partnership, he leaned lower in the saddle, decreased the resistance, seemed to allow the horse to move a step faster. Hell, another dozen miles was a cinch. A snap cinch.

Only three miles out from Gilman Forks Station, coming off another rise, even as he leaned as low in the saddle as he could, he spotted a tree down on the narrow trail, and a shadow moving out of sight like rabbit ducking from a hawk.

"Oh, boy," he said to his horse, if nobody else. "I wonder what I'm carrying, looks like someone else wants it. I might not be so lucky this time." The boy's contorted face came back to him, and his words ... "Hurry, I'm sworn." "Hurry, I'm sworn."

Danby looked to his left and saw no way out. On his right he saw a break in some low climbing hills. Marking the sign, a distant peak he seemed to be aiming at for the last few miles, and the sun as it hung in its path, he swung his horse into that climb and left the trail that promised to be accompanied by no-good-at-all. It was a moment of doubt until he heard the sound of several shots and bullets hitting near him. In good fortune for him, the horse was an excellent climber, and powered his body up and over the first rise, and then another, until a level run for a hundred yards or so lay out in front of him. Spurred, the horse leaped at that easy run and put much space between him and the who-evers back there.

When horse and rider broke free of a stretch of trees after the open run, Danby saw more grass and trail ahead of him. And the peak in the distance and the hanging sun told him he was right on the mark.

After ten miles of hard riding, he saw Mercy Creek Station ahead of him, and the scene back at Gilman Forks Station seemed to be repeating itself ... a man stood waving him on and a horse was standing beside him.

"Where you been, son? I've been waitin' on you. You must be new, as I don't reckon I've seen you before."

"You ain't seen me before. One rider was shot by robbers lookin' for this. I just took his place. I'm off the Hayes Jackson ranch, just a cowpoke pickin' up and sittin' in for the fella got shot." Danby put his hand on the mochila. "What's in this thing anyway? Gold? Or what? "Sides, there was somebody else back of me a ways who were goin' to have a go at me. Had a tree down on the trail. Just a few miles back."

"Well," the man said, "we have some soldiers in the area and I'll tell them about them varmints. They'll check them out and
122

straighten things out." He stopped talking for a minute, slapped the mochila on the new horse and continued. "The boy goin' to be okay? We ain't lost one that I know of in a whole year. Know his name?"

"The fella at the last station said he expected Kid Hoskins, but I don't know if that's his name. He'll be okay the cook does what he can. I left him at the ranch with the cook. Only one at doctorin' I know."

"Well, son, I'll send word with the next riders both ways, about how you stepped in to help a pony boy. They ought to catch up to you somehow, the folks from Central Overland California and Pikes Peak Express Company, which all other folk around here and elsewhere on the trail call the Pony Express. They owe you."

He slung the mochila onto the new horse and said, "Best be on your way, son. This'll be your last leg. The home station's up there. I know Junior Beckman's waiting ahead to carry on to the next section. Whatever you got in that sack's got to be damned important, for the troops were up to something. So giddy up."

The harsh slap came down on the horse's rump and sit-in pony rider Brace Danby set off on the last leg of his only time of employment by the Pony Express, and official words carried in the mochila on his saddle that served to square California onto the Union for the next several tumultuous years of war.

Me? I'm Brady Cross, the 4th, and I am going to tell you a story told me by my grandfather, Brady Cross, Jr., as told to him by his father, the first Brady Cross in the line that ran from Heatherford, Oklahoma to this old saloon practically on the edge of nowhere, but still in Nebraska.

The voice of the story, if you get what I mean, has never changed since the first telling, which happened to be in a saloon much like this one.

"Listen," my grandfather said, "real careful and with the wax taken out of your ears, 'cause I got a story you all know and you ain't even heard it yet from me. But be warned there ain't no room for misbelievin' 'cause I don't allow it. You all know, or should know by the skin of your teeth, that truth and conviction, as the perfessors call it, come like a good team of horses been ridden together under the same leather for near 10 years or so, and ain't about to be dee-vorced this time."

"We was in the Nebraska Territory, a hundred of us, a hundred or so, maybe more or less as I figure, and bound for the area around Johnson's Ranch, near Peters Creek, where the Pony Express had a station set up there last year. We moved on horseback, too, and wagon and good boots when necessary, and always with a rifle in hand, except some women folk who ended up carryin' knives sharp as good stone could make 'em. Women have a way with knives as you'll come to know 'fore I'm through here."

"Anyways we was lit upon by a crowd of them Indian folk all screamin' like ole ladies and makin' crazy on their horses quick as darts they was, and the one leadin' them was not one a them if you can count the cotton in that kind of stuff. He was I swear as white as yore ma's bread with good flour at the start of bakin' and wore a blue fancy jacket like I never seed on anybody with a belt in the middle that pulled it and him together the way a saddle gets cinched underneath. A knife with a big black handle was stuck in that belt that 'ppeared to me might seriously harm him if it got loose on a bumpy ride on that horse of his. The hat he was wearin', not no pioneerin' hat nor a cowpuncher's hat, was fancy blue too and decked out with a purple band that had yellow stripes and gidgets in it and it was like a hat some of them ole mountain men would laugh

124

at from here to kingdom come and back if you was to drop in on them, from out of the blue sky as they might say."

"This here strange fella kept yellin' out orders and pointin' where most of us was makin' a good stand of it by unloadin' near all at once that sent a kind of wave of minies and bullets and plain all out iron garbage in a burst that took down both horses and men in its sweep. Seems like he wanted to get them Indian folk to come at us in a big wave of their own only they wasn't about to all get kilt that quick. When one of us, maybe me, hit him with a round or a chunk of hot stuff, he was knocked right off his horse and scrambled for another one and was barely able to get his ass up on that animal and lit out with all the others behind him like he was pulling them on a rope, and they was over the hill and outta sight before the smoke got blowed away by the wind."

"We buried one man out there on the grass and he was a lucky one 'cause we had to bury his woman with him, both wearin' an arrow of their own, not a bullet, in the chest like they come outta the same quiver and maybe from the same bow. We put them down side by side, real close like, in a small hole in the ground that was about as deep as hurry can get it so critters wouldn't feast up on 'em, kinda like they was romancin' their way right to heaven, them two."

"And a few men left widows behind them from that fight and carry the memories of the good and the bad all comin' this way."

"Out there on their lonely way to the next stop we left 'em, and hightailed it toward Johnson's Ranch that was maybe fifty or so miles away the map said by measurin' and the only one we had to go by, bein' as not a one of us had been this way afore and didn't know any trail signs, like I could see now if I was right back there stickin' up all over the place to be looked at. And some other sign I didn't read so good either."

Course, I might give a pause here to say that he was giving us a clue for later on, but I'd best save that and get on with the story.

"We was in Johnson's Ranch in a few days and splittin' up from bein' together all that time on the way out here, and some bein' real glad to see some go and some sad at seein' others go on their way to another place in Nebraska or even further closer to the Rocky Mountains and gold or silver waitin' on 'em, and some stayed in Johnson's Ranch and I guess are still there planted, like some that was hopin' to get growed again like some folk think, kind of across

125

the big divide but bein' themselves all over again. But some knowin' they'll come back as a cougar or a deer swift as lightning or a goat up on the side of a mountain looks like he's 'bout as near to God as any of us'll ever get.''

"And it's all of five years later and I'm comin' back to Johnson's Ranch, to a spread my brother Jagar owns, 'cause I've been out and back a number of times and I'm sittin' in the saloon one night mindin' my own business and really likin' the way my throat's feelin' when a fella walks in and looks around and takes a seat at a far table and gets downright comfortable for a stranger and orders a drink from one of the ladies tendin' the house and he's wearin' that same damned silly blue hat with the purple band and funny gidgets in it along with the stripes that I saw out on the trail and I'm tinglin' all over all of a sudden and bein' unnaturally noticeable while I'm doin' it and Jagar says, 'What's the matter with you, Brady, 'cause you look like you seen a ghost? I thought you was goin' to drop your drink in the middle of finishin' it off.'''

"The bartender was right near then, and was one of them old hands from back then, and his name was Oliver Crowne and he says, 'Don't think your brother's seen a ghost, Jagar. I seen him too, that fella with the Funny Hat down there just startin' in to get his throat some dampened. What do we do now, Brady?' And he poured each of us another glass and sat back and waited, him bein' one of them kind always waitin' on someone else to do the business, like ask for a drink usually, not pour it 'forehand or don't get to mixin' in stuff don't pay enough to do so up front. Not if your life was to depend on it.''

"But I don't carry no gun like I was a gunfighter, 'cause my hands are slow and clumsy and belong more on a shovel or a hammer and would be awful late gettin' a gun out of a holster tied down on my hip, but them hands is as hard as rocks and ain't never broke under or from anythin' and all I need is a chance to hit somethin' and it ain't never goin' to hit back, never again.''

"So I'm on my slow, meanderin' way down to introduce myself and I seen this gent beside the door with his hand inside his coat and he's real nervous like there's a gun attached to that nervous hand of his and he's part of Funny Hat's troupe. I don't like bad odds, so I turnt around and went back and said to Jagar, 'You go make sure that nervous fella at the door don't step into the middle of what's between me and Funny Hat, which is some serious, like you might tap him on the back of the head as you're gonna leave here all done with drinkin' for the time bein'.'"

"And Jagar, like the quick cat he is and not all clumsy as a bear like me, slaps the fella on the side of the head with his gun and grabs him easy and walks easy and cozy out the door like he's hauling hay into the barn and practic'lly nobody notices anythin' includin' Funny Hat and I make my way again like I was goin' in the first place and I ain't got a itch in my fingers like a fast gun must have but I could feel the power buildin' up in my fists like the iron I said was there. I was almost to the table where he's sittin' and another fella I never even seen and who's sittin' right beside me as I walk by, says to me as he stands up, 'Say fella, do I know you?' And I figure he does and is one of Funny Hat's crowd and I slammed him aside the head and he goes down like a rock's hit him and Funny Hat stands up and is about to get his gun when quick as a cat Jagar belts him on the side of the head like he's already done to one of them, and Funny Hat lies across the table where his drink is all spilt."

"Someone in the crowd, maybe another of Funny Hat's folks, whether he's tempted, pushed or challenged, fires off a shot and it must have gone down at the floor 'cause nothin' or no one gets hit and nothin's broken but silence."

"Of course, there's all kinds of noise and commotion goin' on, and people runnin' back and forth and someone runnin' for the sheriff and I sit at the table and wait for law and good works to come and visit the scene."

"Then someone shoots from the doorway and Jagar, at the end of the bar, shoots and there's a scream from outside and it's the mother of a kid who's been hit and kilt on the spot. When the sheriff comes in in the middle of all the ruckus and hears the stories as folks sit back down to drink, he arrests Jagar and says he's gonna charge him with murder as a bunch of folks say the only one they saw shoot was Jagar."

"They call the judge and court comes into the place and the jury's put in their place and witnesses answer the sheriff's questions and it all points to Jagar, and one gent says, 'I was outside when the shooting started in here and everybody in the street looked at this place like it was going to blow up or come apart with gunfire and then the kid falls down and the mother screams,' and the mother's in the court and says, 'He killed my son,' and she points right at Jagar and she's madder'n that hen got caught in the rain."

"The judge says, 'It plain looks to me, Jagar, that you killed the boy even if it was an accident, and I'll have to send you off to jail.'"

"Then, right there in the middle of court, a couple of wild things happen and one gent tries to run out and a few gents grab him, wonderin' where he's goin' in such a hurry and Doc Mederson says, 'I got a question, Judge, because the witness said that everybody outside was looking at the saloon here when the ruckus was going on.' 'So?' said the judge.' And the doc says, 'Then how come the boy was shot in the back?' And the judge says, 'Case closed, Jagar. You can go home tonight after we get drunk a bit. And I want to know where this fellow was when the shooting started, the one who wanted out of here in a big hurry.' And the storekeeper jumps up from his table in the corner and says, 'He was standing outside my store right on the corner of the alley and he had his rifle out like he was going to have it cleaned, like he was plain studying it.' And the judge says, 'Say, Doc, was it a rifle shot that killed the boy and you can swear to your answer?' And the doc says, Sure can do.'"

"And it was all over just like that."

Of course, down the line somewhere, a few details came to light and Funny Hat in the beginning had escaped from a long prison term and formed a band of bad guys who traveled as a gang when they wanted to and as single agents when they were directed by Funny Hat to gain any edge on opponents or targets.

The good word has it that two women recognized a couple of them one time a few years later outside a store in the next town and invited them to "our own little private-like campsite out in the foothills if you know what we mean" that was not anything of the sort, and sliced them up pretty bad with knives must have been saving forever. One gent says there's more than two women with long-memory knives sitting not too far from here, and that ought to make a few strangers uncomfortable if they are recognized and set on by women with the long-knives, because even the best butchers learn from their mommas how to cut the steak nice and properly.

And that first Cross relative of mine telling the story sort of looked into the eyes of his listeners and must have made a few men shake, especially thinking about mistaken identity.

Life had its full range of artillery out for him, front and center. *Oh, Death of the Pale Rider* sounded anew in the silence of Briggs Thornton's mind, even as the day bore itself harsh as a frozen thunderbolt, a huge icicle with breath and as cold as the bank was to his latest overture. Around his neck the wrap of a muffler was not a comfortable wrap, feeling it a trade-off of an itch to keep the chill off his nape.

Adding to all his misery, Humboldt was sick, the stallion not going to make it out of the barn on his own, not on those great legs for sure. And the ground now frozen at least two feet down. Briggs Thornton didn't know how he was going to bury Humboldt, if it came to that, though everything pointed to his death. It would be like setting in a new gasoline tank, all that digging. Not selling that great animal for glue or meat was a certainty, but the weather was dropping a degree an hour and would sock the earth into more solid granite, Mother Earth's deep-poured concrete. Keeping that worry company was the other onus working on him, the responsibility of getting Dabney Overton, his last ranch hand, settled someplace, not appeasement but settlement, not payment but duty, for the old ramrod was so owed. A seventy-year old man doesn't just up and move on from where he's spent fifty years of his life, no matter how mouthy he was getting. Of late the ranch hand's impatience with Briggs' decision-making had become very noticeable. "Sometime when the time comes, boss, it's already gone." And Briggs' wife Mavreen had noted on a number of occasions that the old cowpoke was getting "testy and stretching his mouth too far from the saddle."

The frozen thunderbolt clapped about him again. *Oh, Death of the Pale Rider.*

At the moment Briggs couldn't discern if Humboldt's problem was worse than the foreclosure he was facing, or Dabney's imminent plight. A hundred and twenty years on this New England land were the Thorntons from the old country after the first of them being stashed in a horrible ship's hold for a damnation of a journey. And it had fallen upon him to lose the land they had quested and conquered, land with more than one page of history. This was the place where the first Thorntons fought the Puritans, the Brahmins, as well as the new politics. And here long ago was found the body of Quilkin the

129

Sneak Pirate atop three of his crew in a deep ditch below the cliffs in the north section, cliffs rising as a fortification for the north pasture. The three pirates had been shot in the back, and Quilkin in the face, as if he had shot them in the hole and one of them, not quite gone to sea, had fired back at their killer.

Humboldt, Briggs' own horse for years, was a black giant, with eyes like great greenish-yellow orbs stolen out of a Chinese color scheme. They were readable and you knew he was knowing you, but couldn't say if he enjoyed the company or not. Briggs' father, Jock Taggard Thornton, died thirty years earlier sitting up frozen on Humboldt's sire, the other great black that owned outright those fields the Thorntons claimed. His name had been Manitou the Magnificent. Manitou had brought the old gent back to the barn in the midst of the worst sneak storm in a hundred years, stiff and straight up as a bayonet-stuck rifle he was, marking his death on the battlefield of storms.

Young Briggs, from a kitchen window, knew from the posture of the rider, from his rigid sitting the saddle, that he had heard the last Yeats' poem from his father on the summer porch where the fireflies would dance him off to bed. In all those years, he had not forgotten that silent death, the awful and visible stiffness of the man of tongues, the storyteller. To that scene he had given the title *Oh, Death of the Pale Rider*, the way man and horse made a dim silhouette against the snow-battered barn, a moonish and sparsely colored silhouette at best. But each time out it seemed as though the old man's voice always said the words of the title and not his own voice, not even under his own breath where identity is always found.

Oh, Death of the Pale Rider. The old gent had said it again, as if hung out on a point of the frozen thunderbolt.

But Briggs kept thinking about the great black horse, the eyes wild at times, and he could bring back instantly his own early fright at the size of such creatures, the way they trod the fields massive as a mountain, fearful with height. Horses like Humboldt, in Briggs' young days, filled the barn door like some colossus out of Egypt or Rhodes he'd only seen in picture books.

"You'll have to truck him out somehow," his wife Mavreen said as he entered the kitchen, swinging her hair up in a gesture, all the punctuation she needed to stress her adjudication. "Get him out of here before he freezes up and in the spring rouses flies and

130

maggots." Mavreen had not been on a horse yet, after eight years of marriage. That had been a minute difficulty at first; Briggs' first wife Julia Rose had fallen from horseback and been impaled on a broken shovel handle. She had walked to a nearby road, holding onto the shovel handle, and collapsed in front of a car coming over the hill. She was dead long before she arrived at the hospital. Mavreen, in turn, was insensitive to horses of any kind, yet her shape was still thin and curvesome and her skin glowed with a rosiness that five-mile walks returned to her. At times Briggs was convinced her only care-giving was in bed. It was not fair, he thought, but it might be true. Glory be in the truth, he smiled sub-vocally, letting part of an argument fall away.

Clad in a puffed denim down jacket, Briggs had come into the kitchen for coffee, and a sheen of silver rode his hair as if the frost had touched it with a wand. His eyes were dark and brittle and a moment of the cold had come with him, sweeping under Mavreen's skirts, and bristling in its rise to touch the back of her neck. He saw her shiver, offered her his coffee. She smiled back, "You can't duck it, Briggs. We got troubles piling on us. I know you love that animal, but he's going to make more trouble, mark my words."

Briggs, at minute evasion, felt like musing. "The old gent must be rolling over in his grave or raising hell among the clouds. Might be paying us back in a new storm. Forecast is unsettled but it looks like snow, even this cold."

"I'm talking about the bills, Briggs. They just don't go away when you talk about something else. Even if you sell the stock we have left, we can't pull ourselves out of this one. I know you're worrying about Dab, too." She tossed her hair again, as much a gesture of futility as she could muster in the face of the man she loved but whose horses she wouldn't ride for love nor money. "I won't tell you what he said yesterday."

"Don't gunnysack me, Mav. Don't add on to it. I'm not struggling to realize what's at us. I've been hard at it for months. I wanted to sell off a smaller piece, but it's like heaven or hell's been arranged against us."

"Or Danton Oliver at the bank has arranged it so that no one comes forward with an offer. He's sworn to get this land. We've known that for a long time. I think he's spent a long time arranging us behind the eight ball, and you keep getting hung up on a horse.

131

My god, Briggs, you lost one wife to a horse." Her mouth hung open, full of her own surprise. The chill touched her again.

The knife-edge of that implicit statement slipped under Briggs' skin. "Mav, you always knew and still know that what counts first with me is loyalty. That great horse out there," and he nodded to the barn, "has earned his way through life. He has supported us every inch of the way and I'll be damned to see him cut up for glue or meat just so we can get him out of here at the least cost to us. He's earned his way!" As if in agreement with Briggs' promise, the wind shifted around and came directly out of the northeast and banged against the windows and the walls of the old homestead. Someplace a board was loose and slapping at its connection and the sound of a barn door slamming boomed like a chunk of thunder. "And Dab counts, just like you say. We can always move on I suppose, but I'm not sure he can. I know he's worried a whole lot more than he shows. His mouth is just part of that."

Briggs sipped his coffee as a signal, put his jacket back on; the motions said *things loose have to be righted.* He welcomed Mavreen into his arms as she said, "I didn't mean it the way it sounded, Briggs. Not really. There's just so much weight coming down atop us. I know what history means to you. The family. The vows. And the promises that people long dead have exacted from you. I'm just so helpless in this. I can't get horses into my blood. It's the way I am."

She wanted to stand on her toes, to look directly into his eyes at his level. "Horses have nothing for me. It is not a sin for me. It's just what I am. And now I'm damn worried about what's going to happen, not to us, but to all of this." Her gesture of widespread hands meant the whole ranch. "My very last gem was in that recent payment." Her fingers were bare, her wrists were bare and he knew her jewelry box was empty. Briggs Thornton drew her tighter than he had in a long while. "I know what you've given up, Mav, but don't give up the last treasure you've got. Don't give up hope." The steel of his arms cut her short of breath and he slipped out the door, each of them sharing the delayed pressure of the other against their bodies.

Leaning against the wind, Briggs saw one barn door slapping loose and a board floating nearly free in a tall fence beside the barn. As the wind blew around him, as the cold continued its hold on the

132

surfaces of all things, his mind kept searching for a solution to the coming problem. Dabney Overton, Briggs' last employee and fifty years at this hitch, stood at Humboldt's stall, his collar tight about his neck, a wool stocking cap down over his ears, age cutting across his face the way lines cut old canvas, eyes calling out an old ramrod's backbone.

"It gets no better, Briggs. Soon's it comes, he goes down like a shot. I've seen it before, like I said yesterday. Davey Warwick's Hellfire went down the same way, like as I said. No name for it but plain tired and life gone out of the blood." Briggs was thinking that Dabney's voice was loaded with messages.

"It's the way some heroes go, Briggs. Just the way they choose. Hellfire was not the horse this one was, but he was a piece, I'll tell you."

"Soon you think?"

"Yuh, all of that. If it's just you and me, we best get him set for the easy move, get him where we can manage him with the tractor." Dabney pointed to the open part of the barn, the finger pointing repeatedly and loaded with enunciation. "Best get him there, under a blanket or two and wait him out. Be a trick or two if I do say." As if to throw that problem under the shadow of another problem, he said, "I have a few hundred dollars in my kit and a few checks not cashed yet. You're welcome to them. This place has been home to me for too damn long. I don't like the thought of leaving it in a huff."

Briggs wanted to put an arm around Dabney's shoulder, but held off. "You and Mav been the best part of me through all this, and you loving horses and her not. Different you are and the same. What I been thinking, Dab, is to drop him at the foot of the cliff and dropping a chunk of it over him. Blast it off with dynamite. That long fissure across the top face has been beaten at by wind and water and the earthchill for a million years now. We might pop enough loose to give him cover forever."

"That's a decent tolerable idea, Briggs. We got some trouble getting Humboldt into the ground where he belongs, but we can sure keep him from the scavengers. There's a whole lot of them out there'd like to tear his carcass to pieces, right to the quick of his bones." At his slight urging, the great horse listlessly moved out of his stall and Dabney threw a blanket over his back.

As he was about to throw the second blanket on him, the yellow eyes of Humboldt turned white and then a lime green and full of shadow, and the great horse crashed to the floor of the barn. The two men could hear a leg bone breaking, caught at the wrong angle, the body athwart itself and falling. There came no other sound but the escape of breath, as if a huge canister emptied itself of air. The wide barn was silent on the inside, only the wind talking on the outside, beating at boards, seeking to whistle its entry. Humboldt allowed one more cavernous sound from his lungs and made silence a fitting gesture, a hero easing off almost by himself. The whole structure of barn board and beam shook down through the fieldstone foundation, and emptiness ensued, a very heady emptiness, as if all things were beholding to death itself, patience being the ultimate acknowledgment.

With chain and rope and a come-along, they got the great horse onto a sled attached to the tractor, Dabney muttering all the time he was setting chain and rope. At last, figuring to have complained long enough, he exclaimed, almost under his breath, about the final demise of the faithful. "Talk about a kick in the hind quarters, this is a one! Sorry, hoss, never believed I'd see it! Get your ass dragging and they drag your ass off!"

Briggs, tying knots, testing them, was trying to understand all the asides thrown at him by the old rider. He felt a crude rawness and cold stabbing at his hands and at his heart, and the muffler failing on his neck again.

In the cold blue air they hauled Humboldt off to the cliff section at the northern end of the ranch, along with a cache of dynamite.

They left the sled with Humboldt atop it against the face of the cliff. Dabney drove the tractor into the copse of cottonwoods standing like a quiver of arrows fifty yards away, his shoulders hanging rounded and sloped. Briggs had not seen the old man like this before. History, he thought, was suddenly catching up to the old rider.

Briggs set up the charges inside the fissure snaking across the front of the cliff. Thirty minutes work in the cold air had him sweating. The picture of his father astride Manitou, the great barn pale behind them, kept entering his mind. He could not shake that eternal picture or the sounds coming with it, *Oh Death of the Pale*

Rider. It was neither song nor eulogy, but it was continuous, rhythmic, in tune with the wind doing its work, spiraling the snow along. Then, as if willing to get out from under one image, something in his mind grabbed onto an image of Julia Rose with the shovel handle coming through her stomach. He knew, down into his boots, that he was going to suffer all his history and all of the family's. It was coming at him. In the midst of it all he could see a crowded ship off the coast of Cork, heading for America. The teeming mass below deck was a piece of Cork itself, dark, damp and unsure that trailblazing was ahead of them.

The frigid air was at his sweat, and beads of it froze him into a new consciousness. He counted out the sticks of dynamite he had planted and reaffirmed their locations. Calling out to let Dabney know the blast was soon coming, he heard him yell back. Briggs walked back away from the cliff edge trailing the wire behind him. He hid behind a huge boulder, heard the wind blow around him, could almost feel the thickness of clouds, and fired the charge.

The blast set off a large section of the cliff, as if a plate had separated from the front face, and the whole section dropped as one piece, falling away in slow motion and then breaking up in a thunderous roar. There was a little smoke and less dust. The wind had quieted as if the blast had set it back on its heels. When Briggs walked off the far end of the cliff and down past the copse of trees, he saw the tractor, the face of the cliff broken over what had been Humboldt on the sled. They were completely covered. He did not see Dabney anywhere, but saw one set of tracks in the snow heading back toward the cliff.

Dabney's impatience had won out.

Caught up in the madness of death, *Oh, Death of the Pale Rider* sounding out again for him, Briggs Thornton suddenly noted, on the newly exposed face of the cliff, his father astride a great horse silhouetted against the white of the barn, Julia Rose with the shovel handle coming through her gut, the darkness in the hold of a ship long gone to sea, an old man with his arm around the neck of a big black horse, and the glitter of gold pieces and gems freed from Quilkin the Sneak Pirate's hiding place in the cliff.

He was not sure what his treasure was.

Some days, Sally Purcell knew, the sun wouldn't come up. This was one of those days. Her husband Clint was a week overdue, more or less, and she could hardly stand the worry. The small amount of money he was carrying did not seem to be an attractive gain for robbers in her mind, but how would they know the difference. Word across the range said that at least three small gangs were responsible for many thefts and robberies. And Clint Purcell, man of men, would protect all his goods, small or large, against any foe or thief. Since the first day she met him, at the dance in Jeff and Wilma Calgary's new barn, she knew what he was made of. Five years of marriage, hard work, cutting a home and a ranch into the wide open spaces of the Shag River Range, had not changed her first impressions of him or her knowledge of him.

The loan from his cousin would take care of the ranch mortgage for the foreseeable future, but any dent in it would hurt them.

The weight of this thought would fill her mind as she tried to work her way through the day: watching little Greg, baking, sewing, feeding the animals, brushing down the horses, being her ranch-wife best. Just as she had done through the past six days of worry. The pain of worry was genuine; the expectations almost as real.

Six days, she felt, was forever.

When little Greg yelled from the top of his lungs that a horse without a rider was coming across the wide grass, her heart froze in place. Breath balled up in her throat, or was it her chest? It did not seem fair that she should have to suffer like this, when she had news to tell Clint.

It was early, and Greg had been awake for over an hour, looking out across the corral and the fence lines to the wide spread of grass, the tree line of the river bank that hid the Shag River, and the mountains on the far side. His pony Almond was in the corral fidgety as usual, the way he saw him each day, knowing the pony was waiting on him. Just like he'd been intent on being the first one to see his father coming home.

But his father's horse was coming across the grass, and he wasn't riding that horse.

"That's Papa's horse, but he isn't on it." He was scrambling

136

down from the loft where he had been sleeping for almost a year after his father had cut a window into the peak so he could look out over the corral and the range beyond. His blond hair curled over his brows and his ears, and hung thick on his neck. His mother was not in any hurry to cut those locks, wanting a child at her apron strings for as long as possible. Now she'd be able to tell her husband that another child was on the way, and little Greg could really start to grow up. He came down the small ladder with definite ease.

But what if something dreadful happened to Clint out there? What would she do with two children? She couldn't afford to even think about that dreadful problem. "I've got to keep my wits about me, and my hopes," she said to herself as she saw how well Greg handled himself on the ladder. "So much like his father," she said, hugging the boy as close as she could.

Trying not to show any alarm, she said, "Let's go rub down that horse of his and give him some water. We can do Almond too. Two horses with one turn," she added, trying to cover her fears, trying not to think about the possibilities. Unhorsed for whatever reason? On the ground somewhere out of sight of the trail? Shot by a bandit and dead on the trail? Perhaps a rattler had startled his horse and threw him and ran off, all the way home, and Clint was out there, walking home? But how could that explain six days late?

She sent word by a passing drummer to the next ranch. An hour later, Craig Mitchell rode up to the ranch house. A big, pleasant man, he moved slowly and surely at all things he did, but she knew he was as dependable as denim.

"You need some help on a problem, Sally? That Thorgren drummer told my wife you needed help. What's going on? What can I do?"

"Clint's late coming back from Foster's Creek. He's carrying a bit of money. He said he'd be gone a few days, more or less, depending on how things went with his cousin in Foster's Creek. Hasn't seen him in a few years."

"Well, how long's he been gone now?"

"I really expected him about a week ago, but his horse came in alone this morning, after sun up."

Mitchell was surprised and said, "Oh, it's time for a little worrying then, I'd guess. Foster's Creek, you say? Well, me and my boys have been going since real early and his horse didn't come past

137

us on the road. We'd have seen him, for sure."

"What's that mean to you, Craig?"

"Must have come across the Tinsley spread, or down through Maddox Pass. I'll get some of my boys, see Tinsley and get a few of his and we'll ride that way back toward Foster's Creek. The ride to Foster's Creek is two days straight through, any way you look at it."

He dropped his hand on Greg's head and rubbed some assurance into the boy. "You and your mom rest easy, Greg. If your daddy's out there on foot for some reason, we'll find him." He patted Sally Purcell on the shoulder, and said, "We'll be back, Sally, soon's we can. Hang in there, girl."

Sally Purcell noticed that when Mitchell must have figured he was out of sight of the ranch, he set off on a gallop. She wondered about that for the rest of the day.

Mitchell and three of his hands rode up to Dell Tinsley, working with two of his sons in the corral between the house and the barn. Tinsley's wife waved from the front door as they rode in.

Tinsley looked up and said, "What brings you and your boys out here, Craig? You got that funny look on your face."

"Clint ain't come home, maybe a week late, as Sally counts it, but his horse rode in this morning all by itself."

"You checked it for sign?" Tinsley said, sure of the reply.

"No blood. No gun sign. Horse looks like it's okay. No hoof problem either."

Tinsley nodded, knowing Mitchell would have not missed a bit of sign, and said, "What trail was he on?"

"That's a question, Dell. His horse didn't come by my place, so I figured we best track back through your spread and up through Maddox Pass. Then on back to Foster's Creek, where he was visiting his cousin."

Tinsley said to his two sons, "Saddle up, boys, and look out there past the cottonwoods for any sign. We'll meet you in Maddox Pass if you don't find anything. Clint's too good a horseman to fall off his horse and he don't drink much to begin with. I'm suspecting somebody had an eye on him."

As an added caution, he said to his sons, "Send one of the other boys to tell the sheriff in town we're out looking for Clint. Tell him about his horse coming home alone, but carrying no signs of trouble. Tell him what trail we'll be on, where we're headed."

138

Five men left the Tinsley ranch headed for Maddox Pass, and two Tinsley sons went off on their range, a hundred yards apart. The sun was high overhead by that time, breaking through a drift of gray clouds.

The Tinsley boys saw nothing beyond the cottonwoods that would alert them to trouble, and were sure that Purcell's riderless horse had not been on that ground. They hastened to catch up with the rest of the party. On the rise to Maddox Pass, the mountain leaping up beside them, one of them spotted two riders coming from back toward town. One brother said, "Has to be the sheriff coming to catch up to us and the others. Didn't take much to get him moving, being so friendly with Clint."

"Heck," the other said, "He's another Blue Army Boy like Pa and Clint and the others. They find Clint okay somewhere they'll have another reunion like that time at Charity Hill we always hear about, all of them meeting after the war was over and all on the way home. Sounded like some wing ding they had that time. It makes me think they won't sit still for much if they find something wrong, if something happened to Clint."

"Yuh," said the other, "and we might be out here for a while."

The other said, "Makes me think the only thing up Maddox Pass way where Clint might be laid low is that cabin old man Sweetser had way back. That's the only cover up there I ever saw. Ain't seen it in a few years, so I don't know what it looks like now. I don't know of one cave up there deep enough to crawl into to get away from trouble or whatever."

"Have to tell Pa and them about it."

All the party, without finding much in their searching after spreading out and going in many directions, had gathered at the high point of Maddox Pass, where they had a view of the river on one side and a good 50 miles of grass on the other side. All the men had come together except the sheriff.

Tinsley said, "Where'd Mark go, Craig? He's always a late arrival. Be late for his funeral if he had his way."

"Wouldn't we all?" Mitchell said, then added, "He's about the most studious man I ever saw when he's tracking. He caught up with that hombre who robbed the bank at Bristol Bend way last year because he saw one damned scratch on a chunk of rock. Man has eyes like an eagle."

139

The searchers stood around, gabbing, holding the reins of their mounts. The wind whistled off the top of the palisade and echoed in the depths of small canyons that were formed in another time and by other forces they did not know existed.

Mitchell wanted to go off looking for the sheriff, when he appeared from one of the smaller box canyons, a look of surprise set on his face.

"Something happened back in there a ways, gents. Some rousting around, with horse tracks, some boot tracks, but disappearing on the rocks. I don't know what it was but I'll guarantee you it had something to do with Clint."

"You saying you're sharp as you ever were, Mark?" Tinsley said, nodding his head in agreement with himself.

"Not a bit, Dell. It was Clint did it, him scratching on a rock with something sharp. His initials. CP as plain as day to me. So I think he was on the ground, probably knocked down, that means there's more than one other man. Clint did not have his gun in hand, else he'd have used it. Took advantage of them, though, when they were probably talking things over, and scratched his initials so we could have a starter on tracking. Plain as day it is."

The youngest Tinsley boy said, "Me and my brother had talked about something like that, Sheriff. Do you know that little cabin old man Sweetser had way back when? It's up in one of them box canyons, right near the end, up against the cliff. Couple of trees hiding it the last time I saw it, like a few years back when Pa didn't know we hung around up here."

Tinsley shook his head as if he had been caught being a bad father.

"Well," the sheriff said, "I never saw the place, but if you can tell us the lay of the land, what kind of cover we might have, I'd suggest we go in there and take a look. I sure can't think of a better place to start, but we know now that something started right near here, and Clint was giving us a good lead with his initials. The man was always a thinker. We knew that way back when war was all around us."

The Tinsley boys described the Sweetser layout as best they could from younger memories, a plan was discussed, and as evening settled in on them they were about to slip inside the canyon.

It was the sheriff who first noticed the smell. "Catch that on

140

the air, gents? That's somebody running a fire and cooking something on it. They may be settling in for the night, so we might have a little bit of edge on them, if that's them." For a moment, the way someone measures what he has just said, he added, "We have another thing on our side; Clint's in the mix and if someone's coming at them from out here, he'll sure figures it's us. That's something on our side. Now let's do it like we discussed, and no heroes. We had enough of heroes in the old days."

Three old hands at war went at their task as quiet as ghosts, approaching the cabin where a light burned in a single window. Not a horse neighed or snorted, and when one man came out of the cabin to investigate a stone tossed lightly against the cliff, he had the snout of a Smith & Wesson stuffed in his mouth, and a whisper said in his ear, "How many more of you are in there? " A jab came on the gun barrel as the man held up one finger. "Is our pard in there too?"

He nodded his head as the jab was repeated, almost at the back of his throat.

"Nice and calmly," came a whisper. "Call your pal out proper for us." The jab came again, just as deep, and then the gun barrel was withdrawn, and placed against his ear.

"Harry, come look at this," he said in what was his most normal voice.

Harry had two guns on him without a tussle, one at his ear, another at his back. "Don't do anything silly, Harry. It'll only hurry you off to the Gates of Hell."

Purcell said, "Glad to see you again, boys. These skunks didn't believe I had no money on me. Kept asking me where it was and I wouldn't tell them because I stuffed it in my bedroll on the horse, but I couldn't tell them that because I could see them going to the ranch looking for it, and I didn't want that."

"You were too slick with them, Clint," the sheriff said, "including marking your initials on the rock. That steered us here."

"Yeh," Purcell said, "slick enough to let them get the drop on me, even when I spotted them earlier and knew I had to hide the money. My horse bolted on them and kept going downhill. They knocked me around a bit after that, but didn't get a penny of it."

"Mom," little Greg Purcell said from his morning watch at the loft window, "there's some horses running across the grass and they're coming our way."

141

He scrambled down the ladder faster than he ever had.

She wondered how she would tell him he was going to be a big brother sometime in the winter.

How would she tell Clint he'd be a father, if he was the next man to come through the door? She'd wait for that problem to develop, and sat in her chair the way a woman might wait for things to happen.

Thomas F. Sheehan served in the 31st Infantry, Korea, 1951-52, and graduated Boston College, 1956. Books include *Epic Cures; Brief Cases, Short Spans; The Saugus Book; This Rare Earth & Other Flights; Ah, Devon Unbowed; Reflections from Vinegar Hill.* eBooks include *Korean Echoes (nominated for a Distinguished Military Award), The Westering,* (nominated for National Book Award)*;* from *Danse Macabre* are *Murder at the Forum, Death of a Lottery Foe, Death by Punishment, An Accountable Death and Vigilantes East. A Collection of Friends, From the Quickening, In the Garden of Long Shadows, The Nations, Where Skies Grow Wide, Cross Trails* and now *The Cowboys* were published by Pocol Press, and *Six Guns, Inc.,* by *Nazar Look,* in Romania. Sheehan has multiple works at these sites: *Rosebud, Linnet's Wings, Serving House Journal, Copperfield Review, KYSO Flash, La Joie Magazine, Soundings East, Literary Orphans, Indiana Voices Journal, Frontier Tales, Western Online Magazine, Provo Canyon Review, Nazar Look, Eastlit, Rope & Wire Magazine, Ocean Magazine, The Literary Yard, Green Silk Journal, Fiction on the Web, The Path, Faith-Hope and Fiction, The Cenacle, etc.* Sheehan's tales have produced 30 Pushcart nominations, and five Best of the Net nominations (and one winner) and short story awards from *Nazar Look* for 2012-2015. *Swan River Daisy* was recently released by KY Stories and *Back Home in Saugus*, 200 pages, 90,000 words, and a chapbook, *Small Victories for the Soul*, are on proposal. (His Amazon Author's Page, Tom Sheehan -- is on the Amazon site.)

www.ingramcontent.com/pod-product-compliance
Lightning Source LLC
Chambersburg PA
CBHW011524240626

47154CB00009B/2950

* 9 7 8 1 9 2 9 7 6 3 6 9 6 *